# Sherlock Holmes Short Stories

*by*

## Sir Arthur Conan Doyle

*Selected and simplified,*
*with Introduction and questions, by*
*Anthony Laude*

Longman

# Contents

# Introduction

When he began writing these stories Arthur Conan Doyle (1859–1930) was a young doctor who had recently given up medicine for literature. He had already written several books, including two Sherlock Holmes novels, and the foundation in January 1891 of the *Strand Magazine* — with a circulation in the hundreds of thousands — gave him the idea of a series of short stories that would carry on the adventures of Holmes and his friend Doctor Watson. The result, ultimately, was a series of fifty-six stories and two more Holmes novels, all published in the *Strand* between 1891 and 1927.

The *Strand* was an extremely up-to-date magazine, bursting with stories, articles and illustrations in which the technological wonders of the time were admiringly depicted, with special emphasis on the achievements of the English-speaking nations. Arthur Doyle and his super-scientific detective hero fitted perfectly into this frame. When the magazine's roving interviewer Harry How visited Doyle during a gap between stories, he began his report with the words:

> Detectivism up to date — that is what Dr Conan Doyle has given us.

How saw Doyle as a typical wholesome sporting Briton:

> He is just a happy, genial, homely man; tall, broad-shouldered, with a hand that grips you heartily . . . He is brown and bronzed, for he enters liberally into all outdoor sports — football, tennis, bowls, and cricket . . .

Doyle the sportsman was as up-to-date as it was possible to be:

> In exercise he most leans towards tricycling. He is never happier than when on his tandem with his wife, and starting on a thirty-mile spin . . .

To Arthur Doyle, Sherlock Holmes was just one minor, often

rather tiresome activity among the many that filled his life, and more than once he tried to escape from him. But the *Strand* and its readers would not tolerate this, and even after Doyle had "slain" his hero he was persuaded to bring him back for more adventures.

Like most writers, Doyle nourished his creative imagination from two broad sources: life and literature. First of all, there were his memories of his old Edinburgh University teacher Joseph Bell, a man whose diagnostic skills went far beyond mere medical facts: he repeatedly astonished his patients and students by the accuracy of his deductions, which were very much like those that Sherlock Holmes makes about the pawnbroker Jabez Wilson near the beginning of "The Red-Headed League". And for the two contrasting personalities of his heroes Doyle had only to look inwards, for he had the essence of both Holmes and Watson in his own character. As Harry How's description will have suggested, in externals he was a Doctor Watson rather than a Sherlock Holmes. "I have often been asked," Doyle himself wrote towards the end of his career,

> whether I had myself the qualities which I depicted [in Sherlock Holmes], or whether I was merely the Watson that I look . . . A man cannot spin a character out of his own inner consciousness and make it really life-like unless he has some possibilities of that character within him . . . [I] have several times solved problems by Holmes's methods after the police have been baffled. Yet I must admit that in ordinary life I am by no means observant . . .

The most important of the literary sources that he drew on when he created the partnership between Holmes and Watson was a group of three stories dating from the 1840s by the American writer Edgar Allan Poe. The hero of these is an eccentric French detective called C. Auguste Dupin, who sets up house in a dilapidated old mansion in Paris with his friend the narrator (a "Watson" character who, however, is so colourless that we never learn his name). Their way of life has all the "decadent" artificiality of the traditional Romantic pose.

They live completely cut off from the world, spending the hours of daylight in darkened rooms, dreamily reading and writing by the feeble light of scented candles, until the clock tells them that true darkness has arrived. They then go out into the night they so much love.

When Sherlock Holmes and Doctor Watson set up home together at the beginning of the first Holmes novel *A Study in Scarlet* (1887) it is all far more English and matter-of-fact. Watson is living by himself in a London hotel, struggling to make ends meet on his small pension after being invalided out of the army. He hears that a scientifically-inclined person named Holmes needs someone to share an attractive set of rooms he has just found. The two men are introduced to one another and agree to take the rooms, which consist of "a couple of comfortable bedrooms and a single large airy sitting-room, cheerfully furnished". The landlady is called Mrs Hudson, and the address (actually a non-existent one) is 221B Baker Street.

Eventually Watson learns that his companion earns his living as a consulting detective, and at the end of the second book about Holmes (*The Sign of Four*, published in 1890) Watson marries one of Holmes's clients. This is the reason why, in the first three of our seven stories, he is not living in Baker Street with Holmes. Sometime between "The Engineer's Thumb" and "The Resident Patient" his wife dies and he comes back and joins his friend in the old rooms. Later Holmes even secretly buys Watson out of his medical practice in order to secure his company full-time at Baker Street.

A century has now passed since the first of the stories were published in the *Strand Magazine* and Sherlock Holmes and Doctor Watson are as popular and fascinating as ever. Part of the attraction, of course, is a "period" richness that comes from the very up-to-dateness we noted above. These stories are steeped in the atmosphere of the 1890s, even though some of them were in fact written in the 1920s. Apart from the telephone that has now been installed at Baker Street, "The Three Garridebs" (*Strand Magazine*, January 1925) has exactly the atmosphere, and very nearly the plot, of "The Red-Headed League" (August 1891). The very free use of telegrams in many of the stories, such as "The Adventure of Wisteria Lodge" (September and October 1908), is very evocative of the earlier period. The strong sense of gentlemanly cosiness and ease that the reader so often gets from the openings of the stories is another important element. The world depicted here is a more stable, more reassuring one than our own.

But the survival of these stories is due above all to Doyle's vivid and credible portrayal of his two central characters and their relationship. This he does largely through dialogue, of which in his rather formal way he is a master.

The eccentric genius yoked to the embodiment of ordinariness: such is the literary formula used by Doyle and by many other writers. But none of the others has ever used the formula more successfully than Doyle does in his sixty-story saga of Holmes and Watson. He not only effectively contrasts the pair, but explores their interaction most imaginatively.

Sherlock Holmes knows his own intellectual and professional worth and has no false modesty about it. Like many exceptionally intelligent men, he is sometimes impatient with the comparative slow-wittedness of those around him. Naturally Watson is the chief sufferer. But he nearly always accepts his lowly role of biographer and assistant humbly and willingly, for to him Holmes is "the man whom above all others I revere". As for Sherlock Holmes, he is a man of habits and Watson has become one of those habits. Holmes enjoys thinking aloud in his presence, and Watson's comparative slowness stimulates as well as irritates his finer mind. But Holmes is not merely the human calculating-machine that he often seems. The other side of his relationship with Watson is illustrated by a touching scene near the end of "The Three Garridebs", where Watson has a momentary glimpse of the depths of true friendship behind Holmes's cool, ironic façade.

# The Red-Headed League

One Saturday morning in autumn, I went to see my friend Sherlock Holmes at his rooms in Baker Street. But he already had a visitor — a very fat old man with unusually bright red hair and a red face — and I therefore said:

"I will go away, Holmes — you are busy." I was apologising for the interruption when he pulled me into the room and closed the door behind me.

"You could not possibly have come at a better time, my dear Watson," he said welcomingly.

"I was afraid you were busy," I said.

"I *am* busy, Watson — very busy."

"Then I will wait in the next room."

"Certainly not!" Holmes turned to his other visitor. "Doctor Watson has helped me in many of my most successful cases, Mr Wilson, and I have no doubt that he will be very useful to us in this one too. Watson, this is Mr Jabez Wilson."

The fat gentleman half got up from his chair and bowed to me, giving me a quick, questioning look from his deep-set little eyes. Then we all sat down.

"Please begin your account again for Doctor Watson, Mr Wilson," said Holmes. "Do not leave out any of the details, which are all very interesting. Yours is an extremely unusual case."

Mr Wilson took a dirty old newspaper out of his pocket, and began to look among the advertisements in it.

Holmes saw me watching the old man and guessed my thoughts.

"You are trying to be a detective, Watson!" he said. "Well, Mr Wilson's appearance proves what his past life has been. It is clear that he has been a workman, that he has been writing a great deal recently, and that he has been in China."

Mr Wilson was quite astonished. "But I had not told you any of those things, Mr Holmes!" he said. "How did you know, for example, that I had been a workman? You are right about that — when I was a young man I was a carpenter."

"Your hands prove it, Mr Wilson," Holmes answered. "Your right hand is much larger than your left. You have worked with it, and so it is more developed."

"But how did you know that I had been writing a lot recently?"

"I looked at your sleeves. The right sleeve is nearly worn out at the wrist, and the left one is nearly worn out at the bend of the arm. Your right wrist and your left arm have been rubbing on a desk. So you must have been writing."

"And how did you guess that I had been to China?"

"On your right wrist you have a tattoo of a pink fish. That particular kind of tattoo is done only in China. I have studied tattoos, Mr Wilson: in fact I have written a book about them. I can also see a Chinese coin on your watch chain. So it was very easy to guess that you had been in China."

Mr Wilson laughed loudly. "And I thought you had done something clever!" he said.

"I ought not to have explained!" said Holmes to me. "Well, Mr Wilson," he went on, "have you found that advertisement yet?"

"Yes, I have found it now." He pointed with a thick red finger to a place in the newspaper. "There it is, sir," he said to me.

I took the paper, which was two months old, and read the following advertisement:

THE RED-HEADED LEAGUE. A man is needed for a new post in this League which was started by the late Ezekiah Hopkins, of Lebanon, Pennsylvania, who left money to the society in his will. The wages are four pounds a week and the work is very easy. Any man who has red hair and good health, and is at least twenty-one years old, may apply for this post. Come to the Red-Headed League's offices, 7 Pope's Court, Fleet Street, London, at eleven o'clock on Monday morning. — DUNCAN ROSS.

"What does it mean?" I said, after I had read this strange advertisement twice.

Holmes laughed happily. "It *is* rather unusual, Watson, isn't it! And now, Mr Wilson, please tell us everything about yourself, your house and servants, and this 'Red-Headed League'."

"Well, gentlemen, I am a pawnbroker in Saxe-Coburg Square, here in London. It isn't a very large business, and makes hardly any profit now. I used to have two men to help me in my shop, but now I have only one. Luckily he is willing to accept half wages, as he wants to learn the business."

"What is the name of this useful boy?" asked Sherlock Holmes.

"His name is Vincent Spaulding. But he isn't a boy. I don't know how old he is. He is an excellent worker, Mr Holmes. He could easily earn much more money in another shop. But I am not going to tell him so!"

"Of course not!" said Holmes. "But has this wonderful person no faults?"

"His only fault is a love of photography. He spends too much time in the cellar, busy with his developing and printing. He is like a rabbit in its hole! But apart from that, he is a good worker."

"And have you any servants?" asked Holmes.

"There is only a fourteen-year-old girl, who cooks and cleans the house. She and I and Spaulding are the only people who live in the house. My wife is dead and I have no children.

"One Monday morning about two months ago, Spaulding came into my office. He had that newspaper in his hand and he said:

"'What a pity my hair isn't red!'

"'Why do you say that?' I asked.

"'Well,' he said, 'here is a new advertisement from the Red-Headed League. If I had red hair I could get a nice easy job and a lot of money.'

"'What is this society?' I asked.

"'Haven't you heard of it?' He sounded surprised. 'It is a

society for men with red hair. You could apply for the post yourself!'

"'What are the wages?' I asked him.

"'Four pounds a week; and the amount of work would be very little. You could easily continue your work here too.'

"Well, two hundred pounds a year would be very useful to me. So I asked Spaulding to tell me more. He showed me the advertisement, saying:

"'I think the society's money came from a very rich American, Ezekiah Hopkins. He was a strange man. He had red hair himself, and when he died all his money went to this Red-Headed League. In his will he gave orders that the money was to be used to give easy jobs to men with red hair.'

"'But thousands of men have red hair!' I said. 'If I applied for the post, I wouldn't have a chance of getting it.'

"'I think you are mistaken, Mr Wilson,' said Spaulding. 'The Red-Headed League gives its posts only to men who were born in London. Ezekiah Hopkins was born here himself, and he loved the old place. And also, only men with really *bright* red hair can get these posts. The society does not accept men with light red hair or dark red hair. You would get the post easily if you applied for it!'

"At last I decided to take Spaulding's advice. As he knew so much about the Red-Headed League, I thought that he would be useful to me at the society's offices. So I told him to shut up the shop and come away with me immediately. He was very willing to have a holiday, and we were soon on our way to Pope's Court.

"Mr Holmes, that little street looked like a basket of oranges! It was completely full of men with red hair of every possible shade. But there were not many who had really bright red hair like mine. Spaulding bent down and pushed his way through the crowd with his head, and pulled me through all those people to the office steps. I could see hopeful men there going in, and disappointed men coming out. Soon we were in the office ourselves.

"There was very little furniture in the room: only two hard chairs, a kitchen table, and a bookcase. A small man was sitting at the table. His hair was even redder than mine. He said a few words to each man who came in, and always managed to find a reason for saying 'No'. However, when it was my turn, the little man was much more friendly. He closed the door, so that he could speak to Spaulding and me privately.

"'This is Mr Jabez Wilson,' said Vincent Spaulding, 'and he is willing to accept a post in the Red-Headed League.'

"'His hair is certainly very fine!' the other man said. 'But is it real? We have been fooled several times before, and have to be very careful.'

"Suddenly he seized my hair in both his hands, and pulled it until I cried out with pain. 'Those are real tears in your eyes,' he said. 'So I will give you the post. Congratulations on your success!'

"He shook me warmly by the hand, and then went over to the window and shouted to the men outside:

"'The right man has now been found! You can all go away!'

"Soon the disappointed men had all gone, and the small man and I were the only people with red hair left in Pope's Court.

"'My name is Duncan Ross,' he said. 'I am the Secretary of the League. We must talk about your new duties now. When will you be able to begin?'

"'Well,' I said, 'that is awkward, as I have a business already.'

"'Oh, don't worry about that, Mr Wilson!' said Vincent Spaulding. 'I shall be able to look after that for you.'

"'What are the hours of work?' I asked Mr Ross.

"'From ten o'clock in the morning until two o'clock in the afternoon.'

"Well, Mr Holmes, most of a pawnbroker's business is done in the evenings. So I could easily work for Mr Ross in the mornings. Besides, I knew that Spaulding was excellent in the shop and would be able to deal with all business matters during the day.

"'Those hours will suit me very well indeed,' I said. 'What is the nature of the work?'

"'First of all,' said Mr Ross, 'you must stay here from ten until two. If you leave the building, you will lose your post for ever. Even if you are ill, you must stay in the office. And the Red-Headed League will not accept any other excuse. Ezekiah Hopkins, who started the society, made all these rules in his will. Your work is to copy out the *Encyclopedia Britannica*\*. There it is, over in that bookcase. You must bring your own pen, ink and paper. Will you be ready tomorrow?'

"'Certainly!' I answered.

"'Well, goodbye, Mr Wilson. I am very glad that you have obtained this important post.' Mr Ross stood up and bowed. Then Spaulding and I went back home. I felt thoroughly delighted at my own good fortune.

"Next morning I bought some paper and returned to Pope's Court, though I had begun to suspect this 'Red-Headed League' was only a joke. However, everything was all right. Mr Ross showed me the beginning of the letter A in the encyclopedia, and then he left. At two o'clock he came back, congratulated me on the amount I had written, and then locked the door of the office after me.

"This continued for more than eight weeks, Mr Holmes. Every morning I arrived at ten o'clock, and every afternoon I left at two. Each week Mr Ross gave me my four pounds in gold. At first he used to come into the office a few times each day, but after a time he did not come in at all. But of course I never left the room, because I did not want to lose my post.

"I copied out the articles on Actors, and Advertising, and Agriculture, and Apples; and many others. I spent a small fortune on paper, and had nearly filled a shelf with my writings. I was even hoping to begin the letter B soon. But suddenly everything came to an end."

"To an end?" said Holmes.

*Encyclopedia Britannica: *a famous encyclopedia*

"Yes, sir. It happened this morning. I went to my work as usual at ten o'clock, but the door was still locked. There was a card nailed to it — a little notice, which I pulled down: here it is."

Mr Wilson showed us a small square card. On it somebody had written:

THE RED-HEADED LEAGUE DOES NOT
EXIST ANY LONGER.
4TH OCTOBER.

Sherlock Holmes and I could not help smiling. "And what did you do then?" asked Holmes.

"I knocked on the doors of all the other offices. But nobody had heard of Mr Duncan Ross. So I went to see the owner of the building, but he too told me that he had not heard of either the Red-Headed League or its Secretary, Mr Ross.

"'Well,' I said, 'who is the gentleman with red hair?'

"'Oh, his name is William Morris. He is a lawyer. But he moved out yesterday.'

"'Where can I find him?' I asked.

"'Oh, at his new offices. He told me the address. Here it is: 17 King Edward Street.'

"I went to King Edward Street, Mr Holmes, but Number 17 is a small factory. Nobody called Morris or Ross worked there, and the manager had never heard of either of them."

"And what did you do then?" asked Holmes.

"I went home to Saxe-Coburg Square and asked Vincent Spaulding to advise me. But he could not give me any useful advice. He only said that Mr Ross would certainly write to me.

"But I was not satisfied, Mr Holmes — I did not want to lose my four pounds a week, and so I came to you."

"You acted wisely, Mr Wilson," said Holmes. "This matter may be a very serious one."

"Very serious indeed!" said Mr Wilson. "I seem to have lost four pounds a week."

"You must not complain, Mr Wilson," said Holmes. "You have really *gained* thirty-two pounds. And do not forget that you have also gained a lot of knowledge about subjects beginning with the letter A! Now let me ask you a few questions. First of all, how long has Vincent Spaulding been working in your shop?"

"For about three months."

"How did he get the post?"

"He answered an advertisement."

"Did any other men apply for the post?"

"Yes: ten or eleven."

"And why did you choose him?"

"Because he seemed to be a sensible young fellow, and he was willing to accept half wages."

"Can you describe him to me?"

"He is small; not thin; he moves quickly. There is no hair on his face, though he is at least thirty years old. He has a white mark just above his eyes."

Suddenly Holmes seemed very excited.

"A white mark!" he cried. "And has he also got little holes in his ears, for earrings?"

"Yes, he has."

"I knew it!" said Holmes. He stood up. "Well, Mr Wilson," he said, "I will think about this matter. Today is Saturday. I hope that everything will be explained by Monday."

When Mr Wilson had gone, Holmes asked me:

"What is your opinion of this Red-Headed League, Watson?"

"I have no opinion, Holmes. It is a complete mystery to me."

"Yes," he said. "I must work hard, Watson."

"What are you going to do?" I asked him.

"First of all I am going to smoke my pipe for fifty minutes. Please do not speak to me during that time." He sat down and began to smoke his dirty old black pipe.

We sat in silence for a long time. I thought Holmes had gone to sleep, but suddenly he jumped up and put his pipe down on the table.

"There is music at the Steinway Hall this afternoon," he said. "Shall we go and hear it?"

"All right," I replied. "I am completely free today."

"Good! Put on your hat, and come. I want to look at Saxe-Coburg Square before we go to the Steinway Hall. And we must also have some lunch. Come along!"

We went partly by the Underground Railway, and partly on foot. Saxe-Coburg Square was a dull, poor sort of place, with some dirty grass in the middle, and a few bushes. I noticed a smell of smoke. The four rows of small brick houses had two floors each, and a cellar. One of them had a shop window and shop door as well as a house door. Above the window we saw a brown board with the name 'JABEZ WILSON' painted on it in white letters. There were also the three golden balls which are the sign of a pawnbroker's shop.

Holmes stopped in front of Mr Wilson's house and looked at it for a moment. Then he knocked loudly several times on the large stones of the street with his stick. Finally he went up to the door and knocked.

The door was opened immediately by a young man.

"Can you tell me the way to the General Post Office, please?" Holmes asked.

The pawnbroker's man did not hesitate for a second. "Go along that street," he said, pointing. "Then go down the third street on the right. After that, the General Post Office is in the fourth street on the left."

"A clever man!" said Holmes, as we walked away. "In my opinion there are only three men in London who are cleverer — and only two who are braver or more daring."

"Did you recognise his face?" I asked.

"My dear Watson, I did not look at his face!"

"Oh! Why then did you knock at the door?"

"Because I wanted to look at the knees of his trousers," Holmes answered. He refused to say anything else about the matter, however, or to explain why he had struck the ground with his stick. He only said: "We have seen Saxe-Coburg Square. Now let us look at the streets behind it."

We left the little square and were soon in one of the noisiest main roads in London. Some of the houses and shops in this main road, however, were separated only by gardens and yards from the quiet little square behind. There was a sweet shop, a newspaper shop, a branch of the City and District Bank, an Italian restaurant, and a small factory where carriages were made.

"We have done our work now, Watson," said Holmes. "Let us have some lunch — and then some music."

As we were coming out of the Steinway Hall Holmes said to me: "I suppose you must go home to your wife now, Watson?"

"Yes, I ought to go home," I replied.

"And I have several things to do myself," he said. "This affair in Saxe-Coburg Square is serious. A great crime has been planned, but I think that we can prevent it. I shall want your help tonight."

"At what time?"

"At ten o'clock."

"I will come to Baker Street at ten," I promised.

"Good! And, Watson, there may be some danger — so please bring your gun." He waved his hand and disappeared into the crowd.

There were two cabs outside the house in Baker Street when I arrived at ten o'clock. Two visitors were there already: a police officer called Peter Jones, and a tall, thin, sad man who was very correctly dressed in dark clothes.

"Watson, I think you know Mr Jones? Let me introduce you to Mr Merryweather, a director of the City and District Bank, who is going to join us in our adventure."

"I hope you are not mistaken in your suspicions, Mr Holmes," Mr Merryweather said. "I have played cards with my friends every Saturday evening for twenty-seven years — this is the first time I have been absent. I do hope you are not wasting my time!"

"I think I can promise you an exciting night, Mr Merryweather," replied Holmes. "You are going to save thirty thousand pounds. And you, Jones, are going to catch a criminal whom you have been trying to find for years!"

"Yes," said Jones: "John Clay, the murderer, forger, and robber. He is only a young man, but he is the cleverest and most dangerous thief in all England. He was not always a robber: he is an Oxford University man, and his grandfather was a king's brother."

Holmes looked at his watch. "It is time to leave now, gentlemen," he said. "Mr Merryweather, will you go with Mr Jones in the first cab, please? Watson and I will follow you in the other one."

It was a long drive, but in the cab Holmes spoke very little. Instead, he sang some of the music that we had heard at the Steinway Hall that afternoon.

At last both cabs arrived at the City and District Bank, in the main road near Saxe-Coburg Square. Using his own keys, Mr Merryweather led us through various doors and along various dark passages. He stopped to light an oil lamp, and then took us into a large cellar, where I noticed a smell of earth. There were many strong boxes in piles.

Holmes took the oil lamp and held it up. "The ceiling, at least, is strong," he said.

"So is the floor," said Mr Merryweather, striking it with his stick. "Oh! It sounds quite hollow!" he cried in surprise.

"Please speak more quietly!" said Holmes. "If the thieves hear us, all our chances will be ruined. Will you please sit down on one of those boxes, and not move?"

Mr Merryweather sat down obediently. He looked a little ashamed. Holmes put the oil lamp on the floor and took a magnifying glass from his pocket. Then, kneeling, he began to examine the cracks between the large stones of the floor.

After a few moments he jumped up and said: "Nothing will happen until midnight. The thieves can do nothing until the old pawnbroker has gone to bed. As soon as he is in bed, however, they will act quickly, in order to gain extra time for their escape."

"What is in these boxes?" I asked.

"Mr Merryweather will tell you that," said Holmes.

"It is our French gold," whispered the director. "These boxes contain thirty thousand pounds, which we borrowed a few months ago from the Bank of France."

"Now, gentlemen, we must wait in the dark," said Holmes, putting out the lamp. "The robbers will soon be here, so we must hide behind the boxes. When they come, we must simply jump on them. They are very dangerous men and we must act quickly. If they shoot at us, Watson, you must shoot at them."

I put my gun on top of a box within reach of my hand.

"There is only one way of escape for them," Holmes continued: "back through the house into Saxe-Coburg Square. Did you do what I asked you to do, Jones?"

"Yes, Mr Holmes. Three policemen are waiting outside Mr Wilson's house."

"Good! And now we must be silent and wait."

We waited for an hour and a quarter, but in the darkness it seemed much longer. My legs became very stiff and tired. I could hear the different breathing of my three companions. Suddenly I saw a little line of light through the floor. Then a large stone was pushed up and the line of light became larger and brighter. I saw a hand appear. But then the stone was quietly let down again and there only the little line of light, along the crack, could be seen.

Then, with much more force, the large stone was pushed up again. It made a loud noise as it turned over on its side. Then a face appeared, and I recognised the man from the pawnbroker's shop. He looked round and then pulled himself up into the cellar. He helped another man to climb out of the hole. Both men were small. The second of them had very bright red hair.

Sherlock Holmes rushed forward and seized the first man, who shouted out to his companion:

"Jump down the hole again, Archie!"

The other man began to climb down. I heard the sound of tearing as Jones seized him by the coat.

The pawnbroker's man had a gun in his hand now, but Holmes knocked it to the floor with his stick.

"You have no chance at all, Mr Clay," he said.

"No: I am caught," the robber replied. "But my friend has escaped — though this police officer has part of his coat in his hand!"

"There are three policemen waiting for your friend outside Mr Wilson's House," said Holmes.

"Oh, indeed? You seem to have done everything very thoroughly," said Clay. "I must congratulate you."

"And I in turn must congratulate you," Holmes replied. "Your idea of the Red-Headed League was very new and effective."

"Give me your hands," said Jones to Clay. "I am going to put the handcuffs on you now."

"Don't touch me with your dirty hands!" said the prisoner. "I am the grandson of a king's brother. You must always say 'sir' and 'please' to me."

"All right, sir," said Jones, smiling. "Please come upstairs with me sir. Then we will get a cab, and take you to the police station."

"That is better," said Clay. Then he bowed to Mr Merryweather, Holmes and me, and walked calmly away with Jones.


"Of course," said Holmes afterwards, "the purpose of the 'Red-Headed League' was not hard to guess. Clay and his companion, the man who called himself Duncan Ross, wanted to get Mr Wilson away from his shop for several hours a day."

"But how did you know that they were planning a bank robbery?" I asked.

"I thought of the shopman's hobby, Watson: photography. Mr Wilson told us that the young man spent too much time in the cellar, busy with his developing and printing. Mr Wilson's description of him made me realise that Vincent Spaulding was really John Clay. Clay was doing something in Mr Wilson's cellar — something that took several hours a day for many weeks. The only explanation was that he was digging an underground passage to another building.

"You wondered why I struck the ground in Saxe-Coburg Square with my stick. Well, I wanted to know whether or not the passage was in front of the house. It was not: the sound my stick made was a dull one, not hollow.

"I then rang the house bell. I did not go into the shop, because I wanted to see the man Spaulding's trousers.

"The knees, Watson, were worn quite smooth, and were very dirty. And they were stained with brown earth!

"When I found out that the City and District Bank was just behind the pawnbroker's house, I knew everything."

"But how did you know that the robbery was planned for tonight?" I asked him.

"Well, when they closed down their 'Red-Headed League' office, that proved that they did not care about Mr Wilson's presence or absence any longer. So I knew that the passage was finished. But they had to use it soon, or else somebody might discover it. And a Saturday would be the best night for them, because the robbery would not be discovered until the Monday morning. So I *knew* that Clay and his friend would come tonight!"

# The Man with the Twisted Lip

Mr Isa Whitney was an opium addict and he could not get rid of the habit. He had once been a fine man, but now people only pitied this bent, unfortunate person with the yellow, unhealthy face. Opium was both his ruin and his only pleasure.

One night in June, when it was almost time to go to bed, I heard the door bell ring. I sat up in my chair, and Mary, my wife, put her sewing down in annoyance.

"A patient!" she said. "At this hour!"

We heard the servant opening the front door and speaking to someone. A moment later the door of our sitting room was thrown open and a lady came in. She wore a black veil over her face.

"Please forgive me for calling on you so late," she began. But then she could no longer control her feelings. She ran forward, threw her arms round Mary's neck, and cried bitterly on her shoulder. "Oh, I'm in such trouble!" she said. "I need help so much!"

"Why!" said my wife, pulling up the visitor's veil, "it's Kate Whitney. You did give me a surprise, Kate! I had no idea who you were when you came in."

"I didn't know what to do, and so I came straight to you."

That was how it always happened. People who were in trouble came to my wife like birds to a lighthouse.

"We are very glad to see you," Mary said. "Now you must have some wine and water, and sit here comfortably and tell us all about it. Or would you like me to send John off to bed?"

"Oh, no, no! I want the doctor's advice and help too. It's about Isa. He hasn't been home for two days. I'm so frightened about him!"

This was not the first time that Mrs Whitney had spoken to us of her husband's bad ways: she and Mary had been at school together. We did our best to calm her down and comfort her.

"Have you any idea where he has gone?" I asked.

"Yes," Mrs Whitney replied. "He's probably at a place called the Bar of Gold, in East London, down by the river. It's in Upper Swandam Street. It's a place where opium addicts go. This is the first time that Isa has spent more than a day there."

I was Isa Whitney's doctor and had a certain influence with him.

"I will go to this place," I said. "If he is there I will send him home in a cab within two hours."

Five minutes later I had left my comfortable chair and sitting room and was in a fast cab on my way east.

Upper Swandam Street was on the north side of the river, to the east of London Bridge. The Bar of Gold was below the level of the street. Some steep steps led down to the entrance, which looked like the mouth of a cave. There was an oil lamp hanging above the door. I ordered the cab driver to wait, and went down the steps.

Inside, it was difficult to see very much through the thick brown opium smoke. The place was a long low room, and was full of beds like those on board a ship, one on top of another. In the half-light I could just see people lying in strange positions on the beds, and little red circles which were the pipes of burning opium. Some of the people were talking softly to themselves. Near one end of the room there was a fireplace, in which a small fire was burning. A tall, thin old man sat there, looking into the fire.

A Malayan servant who belonged to the place came up to me with some opium and a pipe. He pointed to an empty bed.

"No, thank you," I said. "I haven't come to stay. There is a friend of mine here, Mr Isa Whitney, and I want to speak to him."

A man on one of the beds suddenly sat up, and I recognised Whitney. He was pale, untidy, and wild-looking.

"Watson!" he cried. "Tell me, Watson, what time is it?"

"Nearly eleven o'clock."

"On what day?"

"Friday, June the 19th."

"Good heavens! I thought it was Wednesday."

"No, it's Friday. And your wife has been waiting two days for you. You ought to be ashamed of yourself!"

He began to cry. "I was sure I had been here only a few hours! But I'll go home with you. I don't want to frighten Kate — poor little Kate! Give me your hand: I can't do anything for myself. Have you a cab?"

"Yes, I have one waiting."

"Good. But I must owe something here. Find out what I owe them, Watson."

As I walked along the narrow passage between the beds, looking for the manager, I felt someone touch my sleeve. It was the tall man by the fire. "Walk past me, and then look back at me," he said. When I looked again he was still bending over the fire — a bent, tired old man. Suddenly he looked up and smiled at me. I recognised Sherlock Holmes.

"Holmes!" I whispered. "What on earth are you doing in this disgusting place?"

"Speak more quietly! I have excellent ears. Please get rid of that friend of yours. I want to talk to you."

"I have a cab outside."

"Then send him home in it. And I suggest that you give the driver a note for your wife. Tell her you are with me. And wait outside for me: I'll be with you in five minutes."

In a few minutes I had written my note, paid Whitney's bill, led him out to the cab, and said "Good night" to him. Then Holmes came out of the Bar of Gold, and we walked along together. At first he walked unsteadily, with a bent back, but after the first few streets he straightened himself out and laughed heartily.

"I suppose you think I have become an opium addict, Watson!" he said.

"I was certainly surprised to find you in that place," I replied.

"And I was surprised to see *you* there!"

"I came to find a friend."

"And I came to find an enemy!"

"An enemy?"

"Yes, Watson, one of my natural enemies — a criminal! I am working on one of my cases. I fear that Mr Neville Saint Clair entered the Bar of Gold and that he will never come out of the place alive. There is a door at the back of the building that opens onto the river. I believe that many men have been murdered there, and that their bodies have been thrown out through that door. If I had been recognised the wicked Indian sailor who owns the place would have murdered me too! I have used the Bar of Gold before for my own purposes, and have often found useful clues there, in the conversation of the opium addicts. The owner has sworn to have his revenge on me for it." Suddenly Holmes whistled loudly. "The carriage should be here by now!" he said.

We heard an answering whistle in the distance. Then we saw the yellow lamps of the little carriage as it came near.

"Now, Watson, you will come with me, won't you?" said Holmes, as he climbed in.

"If I can be of any use."

"Oh, a friend is always useful. And my room at the Saint Clairs' has two beds."

"At the Saint Clairs'?"

"Yes. I am staying there while I work on the case."

"Where is it, then?"

"Near Lee, in Kent. It's a seven-mile drive. Come on!"

"But I don't know anything about your case!"

"Of course you don't. But you soon will! Jump up here. All right, Harold," he said to the driver, "we shan't need you." He handed the man a coin. "Look out for me tomorrow at about eleven o'clock. Good night!"

For the first part of our drive Holmes was silent and I waited patiently for him to begin.

"I have been wondering what I can say to that dear little woman tonight when she meets me at the door," he said at last. "I am talking about Mrs Saint Clair, of course.

"Neville Saint Clair came to live near Lee five years ago. He took a large house and lived like a rich man. He gradually made friends in the neighbourhood, and two years ago he married the daughter of a local farmer. Neville Saint Clair was a businessman in London. He used to leave home every morning and then catch the 5.14 train back from Cannon Street Station each evening. He had shares in several companies. If he is still alive he is now thirty-seven years old. He has no bad habits; he is a good husband and father; and everybody likes him. He has debts of £88 at present, but his bank account contains £220. So he can't have any money troubles.

"Last Monday he went into London rather earlier than usual. He said that he had two important pieces of business to do that day. He also promised to buy his little boy a box of toy bricks. Now, that same day his wife happened to receive a telegram from the Aberdeen Shipping Company. This informed her that a valuable parcel which she was expecting had arrived at the Company's offices in London. These offices are in Fresno Street, which is off Upper Swandam Street, where you found me tonight. Mrs Saint Clair had her lunch, caught a train to London, did some shopping, and then went to the shipping company's offices. When she came out it was twenty-five to five. She walked slowly along Upper Swandam Street, hoping to find a cab. It was a very hot day, and she did not like the neighbourhood at all. Suddenly she heard a cry, and saw her husband looking down at her from a window on the first floor of one of the houses. He seemed to be waving to her, as if he wanted her to come up. The window was open, and she had a clear view of his face. He looked very disturbed and excited. She noticed that he had no collar or tie on; but he was wearing a dark coat like the one he had put on that morning. Then, very suddenly, somebody seemed to pull him back from the window.

"Mrs Saint Clair felt sure that something was seriously wrong. She saw that the entrance of the house was below ground level: this was the door of the Bar of Gold. She rushed down the steps and through the front room, and tried to go up the stairs which led to the upper part of the house. But the owner — the Indian sailor I spoke of — ran downstairs and pushed her back. The Malayan servant helped him to push her out into the street. She rushed along Upper Swandam Street and into Fresno Street, where she fortunately found several policemen. They forced their way into the Bar of Gold and went upstairs to the room in which Mr Saint Clair had last been seen. There was no sign of him there. In fact the only person in the upper part of the house was an ugly cripple who lived there. Both the Indian and this cripple swore that no one else had been in the first-floor front room that afternoon. Suddenly, however, Mrs Saint Clair noticed a small wooden box on the table and realised what it contained. She tore the lid off and emptied out a great quantity of children's bricks. It was the toy that her husband had promised to bring home for his little boy.

"Of course the rooms were now examined very carefully, and the police found signs of a terrible crime. The front room was a plainly-furnished sitting room, and led into a small bedroom, from which the river could be seen. Along the edge of the river there is a narrow strip of ground which is dry at low tide, but which is covered at high tide by at least four and a half feet of water. At that time of day the river is at its highest point. There were bloodstains on the window sill, and a few drops on the bedroom floor too. Behind a curtain in the front room the police found all Neville Saint Clair's clothes except his coat. His shoes, his socks, his hat, and his watch — everything was there. There were no signs of violence on any of the clothes, and Mr Saint Clair, alive or dead, was certainly not there. He seemed to have gone out of the window — there was no other possibility.

"The Indian had often been in trouble with the police before. But as Mrs Saint Clair had seen him at the foot of the stairs only a few seconds after her husband's appearance at the window, he could not have done the murder. He said that he knew nothing about the clothes which had been found in the cripple's rooms. The cripple himself, whose name is Hugh Boone, must have been the last person to see Neville Saint Clair.

"Boone is a well-known London beggar who always sits in Threadneedle Street, near the Bank of England. He pretends to be a match seller, but there is always a dirty leather cap by his side into which people throw coins. I have watched this fellow more than once, and I have been surprised at the very large amount of money that he receives in this way. His appearance, you see, is so unusual that no one can go past without noticing him. He has a pale face and long red hair, and bright brown eyes. His upper lip is twisted up by the effects of an old accident. And he is famous for his clever answers to the jokes of all the businessmen who go past."

"Is it possible that a cripple murdered a healthy young man like Neville Saint Clair?" I asked.

"Hugh Boone's body is bent and his face is ugly," Holmes replied, "but there is great strength in him. Cripples are often very strong, you know. When the police were searching him they noticed some bloodstains on one of his shirt sleeves. But he showed them a cut on his finger, and explained that the blood had come from there. He also said that he had been to the window not long before, and that the stains on the floor and window sill probably came from his finger too. He refused to admit that he had ever seen Mr Saint Clair, and swore that the presence of the clothes in the room was as much a mystery to him as it was to the police. If Mrs Saint Clair said she had seen her husband at the window she must have been dreaming — or else she was mad! Boone was taken to the police station, still objecting loudly.

"When the water level had gone down the police looked for the body of Mr Saint Clair in the mud. But they only found his coat. And every pocket was full of pennies and half pennies — four hundred and twenty-one pennies, and two hundred and seventy halfpennies. It was not surprising that the coat had not been carried away by the tide. But possibly the bare body *had* been swept away. Perhaps Boone pushed Saint Clair through the window, and then decided to get rid of the clothing, which might give clues to the police. But he needed to be sure that the clothes would sink. So he went to the hiding place where he kept the money he earned in Threadneedle Street, and began by filling the pockets of the coat and throwing it out. He would have done the same with the rest of the clothing, but just then he heard the police coming up the stairs, and hastily closed the window.

"Boone has been a professional beggar for many years, but he has never been in any serious trouble with the police. He seems to live very quietly and harmlessly.

"I have to find out what Neville Saint Clair was doing in that house, what happened to him while he was there, where he is now, and what Hugh Boone had to do with his disappearance. The problem seemed to be an easy one at first, but now I don't think it is so easy.

"Do you see that light among the trees? That is the Saint Clairs' house. Beside that lamp an anxious woman is sitting — listening, probably, for the sound of our horse's feet."

We drove through some private grounds, and stopped in front of a large house. A servant ran out to take charge of our horse. The front door opened before we had reached it, and a little fair woman in a pink silk dress hurried out to meet us.

"Well?" she cried eagerly. "Well?"

Perhaps she thought for a moment that Holmes's companion was her lost husband.

Holmes shook his head.

"No good news?" she asked.

"None."

"But no bad news either?"

"No."

"Well, that's a relief. But come in. You must be very tired. You have had a long day's work."

"This is my friend Doctor Watson. He has been of great use to me in several of my cases. By a lucky chance he has been able to come with me this evening."

"I am delighted to see you," said Mrs Saint Clair, pressing

my hand warmly. She led us into a pleasant dining room where there was a cold supper laid out on the table. "Now, Mr Holmes, I have one or two questions to ask you, and I should like you to answer them truthfully."

"Certainly, Mrs Saint Clair."

"It is your real opinion that I want to know."

"About what?" Holmes asked.

"Do you truly believe that Neville is still alive?"

Holmes did not seem to like this question. "*Truly*, now!" she repeated, looking at him as she leant back in his chair.

"Truly, then, I do not," he answered at last.

"You think he is dead?"

"Yes."

"And that he was murdered?"

"I don't know. Perhaps."

"And on what day did he die?"

"On Monday."

"Then, Mr Holmes, how do you explain this letter that I have received from him today?"

Sherlock Holmes sprang out of his chair. "What!" he shouted.

"Yes, today." Smiling, she held up an envelope.

"May I see it?"

"Certainly."

In his eagerness he seized it from her quite rudely, smoothed it out on the table, and examined it very thoroughly. I looked at it over his shoulder. The envelope was a cheap one, and it had been posted at Gravesend in Kent earlier in the day.

"The handwriting on the envelope is poor," said Holmes. "Surely this is not your husband's writing, Mrs Saint Clair?"

"No, but the letter inside is in his handwriting."

"I see that whoever addressed the envelope had to go and find out your address."

"How can you tell that?"

"The name, you see, is in perfectly black ink, and has been allowed to dry slowly. The address is almost grey — which proves that sand has been thrown on the writing to dry it. The man who wrote this envelope wrote the name first, and then paused for some time before writing the address. The only explanation is that he did not know it. But let us look at the letter! Ah! some object has been enclosed in this."

"Yes," said Mrs Saint Clair, "there was a ring. Neville's ring."

"And are you sure that this is in your husband's writing?"

"Yes — though it's easy to see that he wrote it in a great hurry."

This is what the letter said:

Dearest Olivia, do not be frightened. Everything will be all right. There is a mistake that it will take some time to put right. Wait patiently. — Neville.

"This," said Holmes, " is a page torn from some book. It was posted by a man with a dirty thumb. And whoever closed the envelope had a lump of tobacco in his mouth. Well, Mrs Saint Clair, things are beginning to seem a little more hopeful, but I do not think the danger is over yet."

"But Neville must be alive, Mr Holmes!"

"Unless this letter is the work of a clever forger. After all, the ring proves nothing. It may have been taken from him."

"No, no! That's certainly his own handwriting!"

"Very well. But the letter may have been written on Monday, and only posted today."

"That is possible."

"If so, many things may have happened between the two days."

"Oh, you must not make me lose courage. Mr Holmes! I know that Neville is all right. There is such a strong sympathy between us that I always know when any accident happens to him. On that last morning he cut himself in the bedroom, and I in the dining room knew at once that something had happened to him. I rushed upstairs and found that I was right. Do you think I could possibly not know about it if he had been murdered?"

"But if your husband is alive and able to write letters, why should he remain away from you?"

"I can't imagine!"

"And on Monday he said nothing unusual before leaving home?"

"No."

"And you were surprised to see him at that window in Upper Swandam Street?"

"Yes, extremely surprised."

"Was the window open?"

"Yes."

"Then he might have spoken to you?"

"He might. But he only cried out, as if he were calling for help. And he waved his hands."

"But it might have been a cry of surprise. Astonishment at the sight of you might cause him to throw up his hands."

"It is possible. But I thought he was pulled back from the window."

"He might have jumped back. You did not see anyone else in the room, did you?"

"No, but that ugly cripple confessed that he was there, and the owner was at the foot of the stairs."

"Did your husband seem to be wearing his ordinary clothes?"

"Yes, but he had no collar or tie on. I saw his bare throat quite clearly."

"Had he ever mentioned Upper Swandam Street to you?"

"Never."

"Had he ever shown any signs of having taken opium?"

"No, never!"

"Thank you, Mrs Saint Clair. We will now have a little supper and then go to bed. We may have a very busy day tomorrow."

But Holmes did not go to bed that night. He was a man who sometimes stayed awake for a whole week when he was working on one of his cases. He built himself a nest of cushions and filled his pipe. Then he sat down, crossed his legs, and looked with fixed eyes at the ceiling. I was already in bed and soon went to sleep.

Holmes was still smoking when I woke up next morning. It was a bright sunny day, but the room was full of tobacco smoke.

"Are you awake, Watson?"

"Yes."

"Would you like to come for an early-morning drive?"

"All right."

"Then get dressed! Nobody is up yet, but I know where the servant who looks after the horses sleeps. We shall soon have the carriage on the road!" Holmes laughed to himself as he spoke. He seemed to be a different man from the Holmes of the night before.

As I dressed I looked at my watch. It was not surprising that nobody in the house was up: it was only twenty-five past four. Soon Holmes came back and told me that the carriage was ready.

"I want to test a little idea of mine," he said as he put his shoes on. "I think, Watson, that I am the most stupid fool in Europe. I deserve to be kicked from here to London. But I think I have found the explanation of Neville Saint Clair's disappearance now. Yes, Watson, I think I have the key to the mystery!"

"And where is it?" I asked, smiling.

"In the bathroom," he answered. "Oh, yes, I am not joking," he went on, seeing the astonishment on my face. "I have been there, and I have taken it out, and I have it in this bag. Come on, Watson, and let us see whether this key is the right one."

The little carriage was waiting for us in the bright morning sunshine. We both sprang in, and the horse rushed off along the London road. A few country carts were about, taking fruit in to the London markets, but the houses on either side of the road were as silent and lifeless as in a dream.

"Oh, I have been blind, Watson!" said Holmes. "But it is better to learn wisdom late than never to learn it at all."

In London, a few people were beginning to look out sleepily from their windows as we drove through the streets on the south side of the city. We went down Waterloo Bridge Road and across the river; then along Wellington Street. We stopped at Bow Street Police Station. The two policemen at the door touched their hats to Holmes, who was well known there. One of them held the horse's head while the other led us in.

"Who is the officer on duty this morning?" asked Holmes.

"Mr Bradstreet, sir," answered the man.

A large fat man came down the passage just then.

"Ah, Bradstreet, how are you?" said Holmes. "I'd like to have a word with you."

"Certainly, Mr Holmes. Let us go into my room."

It was a small office, with a desk and a telephone. Bradstreet sat down.

"What can I do for you, Mr Holmes?"

"I am here in connection with Hugh Boone, the beggar — the man who has been charged with being concerned in the disappearance of Mr Neville Saint Clair."

"Yes. We are still busy with that case."

"You have Boone here?"

"Yes. He's locked up."

"Is he quiet?"

"Oh, he gives no trouble. But he's a dirty fellow."

"Dirty?"

"Yes. He doesn't mind washing his hands, but his face is as black as a coal miner's. Well, as soon as his case is settled he'll have to have a proper prison bath!"

"I should very much like to see him."

"Would you? That can easily be arranged. Come this way. You can leave your bag here."

"No, I think I'll take it with me."

"Very good. Come this way, please." He led us down a passage, opened a barred door, and took us down some stairs to another white passage. There was a row of doors on each side.

"The third door on the right is his," said Bradstreet. "Here it is!" He looked through a hole in the upper part of the door.

"He's asleep. You can see him very well."

Holmes and I both looked through. The prisoner lay with his face towards us, in a very deep sleep, breathing slowly and heavily. He was a man of middle height, coarsely dressed in a torn coat and a coloured shirt. As Bradstreet had said, he was extremely dirty. One side of his upper lip was permanently turned up, so that three teeth were always showing. He looked like an angry dog. His head was covered almost down to the eyes with very bright red hair.

"He's a beauty, isn't he?" said Bradstreet.

"He certainly needs a wash," Holmes replied. "I had an idea that he might be dirty, and so I brought this with me." He took a wet towel out of his bag.

"What a funny man you are, Mr Holmes!" said Bradstreet with a hearty laugh.

"Now, Bradstreet, open that door very quietly, please."

"All right." And Bradstreet slipped his big key into the lock, and we all went in very quietly. The sleeping man half turned, and then settled down once more. Holmes stepped quickly over to him and rubbed the towel firmly across and down his face.

"Let me introduce you," he shouted, "to Mr Neville Saint Clair, of Lee in Kent!"

The effect of Holmes's towel was extraordinary. The skin of the man's face seemed to come off like paper, taking the twisted lip with it. Holmes took hold of the untidy red hair and pulled it off too. The ugly beggar had changed into a young gentleman with black hair and a smooth skin. He sat up and rubbed his eyes, looking round sleepily. Then he realised what had just happened, gave a terrible cry, and hid his face.

"Good heavens!" cried Bradstreet. "It certainly is the missing man. I recognise him from the photograph."

By now the prisoner had managed to control himself. "And what," he asked, "am I charged with?"

"With being concerned in the disappearance of Mr Neville Saint ——" Bradstreet began. "But of course you can't be charged with that! Well, I have been a member of the police force for twenty-seven years, and I have never seen anything like this!"

"If I am Neville Saint Clair, no crime has been done. It is clear that you are breaking the law by keeping me here."

"No crime has been done," said Holmes, "but you ought to have trusted your wife."

"It was not my wife that I was worried about. It was the children! I didn't want them to be ashamed of their father. And what can I do now?"

Sherlock Holmes sat down beside him on the bed, and touched his shoulder kindly.

"I advise you to tell everything to Mr Bradstreet," he said. "It may not be necessary for the case to come into court. Your story will probably never be mentioned in the newspapers. Your children need never find out about it."

Saint Clair gave him a grateful look.

"I will tell you the whole story.

"My father was a schoolmaster in Derbyshire, where I received an excellent education. I travelled a great deal after I left school. I was an actor for a time, and then became a reporter on the staff of an evening paper in London. One day I was asked to write a few articles on begging in London. It was then that all my adventures started. I decided that the best way of collecting facts for my articles would be to become a beggar myself for just one day. When I was an actor I had, of course, learned all the skills of make-up, and I now made good use of them. I painted my face and fixed my upper lip in an ugly twist, in order to make people pity me. Red hair and suitable clothes were the only other things necessary. I then placed myself in one of the busiest streets in London. I pretended to be a match seller, but I was really a beggar. I stayed there for seven hours. At home that evening I was surprised to find that I had received more than a pound.

"I wrote my articles, and thought no more of the matter for some time. Then I signed my name on a paper for a friend who wanted to borrow some money; he was unable to pay his debt, and so I found that I owed twenty-five pounds. I did not know what to do. Suddenly I had an idea. I asked for two weeks' holiday, and spent the time begging in Threadneedle Street. In ten days I had paid the debt.

"Well, you can imagine how hard it was to settle down to hard work on the newspaper at two pounds a week, when I knew that

I could earn as much as that in a single day! I had only to paint my face, put my cap on the ground, and sit still. Of course it hurt my pride to do it, but in the end I gave up my post, and sat day after day in the corner I had first chosen. My ugly face made everybody pity me, and my pockets quickly filled with money. Only one man knew my secret. This was the owner of the Bar of Gold in Upper Swandam Street, an Indian sailor. It was there that I changed myself into an ugly beggar each morning, and there that I became a well-dressed businessman again in the evenings. I paid the fellow well for his rooms, so I knew that my secret was safe with him.

"Well, very soon I realised that I was saving money fast. I do not mean that any beggar in the streets of London could earn seven or eight hundred pounds a year, but I had unusual advantages. My knowledge of make-up helped me a great deal, and my clever answers quickly made me almost a public character. All day and every day, the money poured into my cap. I usually received at least two pounds in a day. I was almost a rich man.

"I was able to take a large house in the country, and later to marry. Nobody had any idea where my money really came from. My dear wife knew that I had business in London: that was all.

"Last Monday I had finished for the day, and was dressing in my room in Upper Swandam Street, when I saw my wife outside. She was looking up at me. This was a great shock to me, and I gave a cry of surprise and threw up my arms to cover my face. I rushed downstairs and begged the owner of the place to prevent anyone from coming up to me. Then I ran upstairs again, took off my clothes, and put on those of 'Hugh Boone'. I heard my wife's voice downstairs, but I knew that she would not be able to come up. Hastily I put on my make-up and my false hair. Just then I realised that the police might search my rooms. I did not want my own clothes to be found. I filled the coat pockets with coins, and opened the window. I had cut my finger at home in Kent that morning, and in my haste I opened the cut again. I threw the heavy coat out of the window and saw it disappear into the river. I would have thrown the other clothes out too, but just then I heard the policemen rushing up the stairs. A few minutes later I was seized as my own murderer! But I was relieved that nobody realised who I was.

"I was determined not to be recognised, and so I refused to wash my face. I knew that my wife would be very anxious about me, and I therefore slipped off my ring and found an opportunity to give it to the owner of the Bar of Gold, togethe. with a short letter to her."

"Mrs Saint Clair did not get that note until yesterday," said Holmes.

"Good heavens! What a terrible week she must have had!"

"The police have been watching the Indian," said Bradstreet, "and he must have had great difficulty in posting the letter without being seen. He probably handed it to one of the sailors who come to the Bar of Gold to smoke opium. The man may have forgotten to post it until yesterday."

"I think you are right," said Holmes. "Mr Saint Clair, have you never been punished for begging in the streets?"

"Oh, yes, I have often had to pay some money. But I could easily afford it!"

"Your life as a beggar must stop now," said Bradstreet. "If Hugh Boone appears once more in the streets of London we shall not be able to prevent the newspaper reporters from writing about the case."

"I swear solemnly never to beg again," said Saint Clair.

"In that case you will hear no more of the matter," said Bradstreet. "But if you are ever found begging again, everything will have to be made public. Mr Holmes, we are very grateful to you for your successful handling of the case. I wish I knew how you get your results!"

"I found the explanation of this affair by sitting on five cushions and smoking my pipe all night," answered my friend. "I think, Watson, that if we drive to Baker Street now we shall be just in time for breakfast."

# The Engineer's Thumb

The exciting affair of Mr Hatherley's thumb happened in the summer of 1889, not long after my marriage. I was in practice as a doctor. I often visited my friend Sherlock Holmes at his Baker Street rooms, and I sometimes even managed to persuade him to come and visit my wife and me. My practice had steadily increased, and as I happened to live near Paddington Station, I got a few patients from among the railway workers there. One of these, a guard whom I had cured of a painful disease, was always praising my skill and trying to influence new patients to come to me.

One morning a little before seven o'clock, I was woken by our servant knocking at the bedroom door. She said that two men had come from Paddington Station and were waiting in my office. I dressed quickly and hurried downstairs. I knew from experience that railway cases were usually serious. Before I had reached the office, my old friend the guard came out and closed the door tightly behind him.

"I've got him here," he whispered, pointing over his shoulder with his thumb, as if he had caught some strange wild animal for me. "It's a new patient. I thought I'd bring him here myself, so that he couldn't run away. I must go now, doctor. I have my duties, just as you have." And he was out of the house before I could thank him.

I entered my office, and found a gentleman seated by the table. He was dressed in a country suit, with a soft cloth cap, which he had put down on top of my books. There was a bloodstained handkerchief wrapped round one of his hands. He was young — not more than twenty-five, I thought. He had a strong face, but he was extremely pale, and seemed to be in a state of unhealthy excitement which he could scarcely control.

"I'm sorry to get you out of bed so early, doctor," he began. "But I have had a very serious accident during the night. I came back to London by train this morning, and at Paddington I asked the railway people where I could find a doctor. One good fellow very kindly brought me here. I gave your servant a card, but I see that she has left it over there on the side table."

I picked it up and looked at it. "Mr Victor Hatherley," I read, "hydraulic engineer, third floor, 16A Victoria Street." That was the name of my morning visitor.

"I am sorry you have had to wait so long," I said, sitting down. "Your night journey must have been dull too."

"Oh, my experiences during the night could not be called dull!" he said, and laughed. Indeed he roared and shook with unhealthy laughter.

"Stop it!" I cried. "Control yourself!" I poured out a glass of water for him.

It was useless, however. He went on laughing for some time. When at last he stopped he was very tired and ashamed.

"It was stupid of me to laugh like that," he said in a weak voice.

"Not at all." I poured some brandy into the water. "Drink this!"

Soon the colour began to return to his pale face. "That's better!" he said. "And now, doctor, would you mind attending to my thumb, or rather to the place where my thumb used to be?"

He took off the handkerchief and held out his hand. It was a terrible sight, and although I had been an Army doctor I could hardly bear to look at it. Instead of a thumb there was only an uneven, swollen red surface. The thumb had been completely cut — or torn — off.

"Good heavens!" I cried. "This is a terrible wound. It must have bled a great deal."

"Yes, it did. I fainted when it happened; and I think I must have been unconscious for along time. When I returned to consciousness, I found that it was still bleeding. So I tied one end of my handkerchief very tightly round the wrist, and used a small piece of wood to make it even tighter."

"Excellent! You should have been a doctor."

"I'm a hydraulic engineer, you see: the force of liquids is my subject."

"This has been done," I said, examining the wound, "by a very sharp, heavy instrument."

"An axe," he said.

"It was an accident, I suppose?"

"No!"

"Was somebody trying to murder you, then?"

"Yes."

"How terrible!"

I cleaned the wound and bandaged it. He did not cry out as I worked on his hand, though he bit his lip from time to time.

"How are you feeling now?" I asked, when I had finished.

"I feel fine! Your brandy and your bandage have made me feel like a new man. I was very weak, but I have had some terrible experiences."

"Perhaps you had better not speak of the matter. It upsets you too much."

"Oh no! Not now. I shall have to tell everything to the police. But really, if I did not have this wound, the police might not believe my statement. It is a very extraordinary story and I have not much proof of it. And I doubt whether justice will ever be done, because I can give the detectives so few clues."

"In that case," I said, "I strongly advise you to see my friend Sherlock Holmes before you go to the police."

"Oh, I have heard of Mr Holmes," said my visitor, "and I should be very glad if he would look into the matter, though of course I must inform the police as well. Would you give me an introduction to him?"

"I'll do better than that. I'll take you round to him myself."

"You're very kind."

"We'll call a cab and go together. We shall arrive just in time to have a little breakfast with him. Do you feel strong enough to go out?"

"Oh yes! I shall not feel comfortable in my mind until I have told my story."

"Then my servant will call a cab, and I shall be with you in an instant." I rushed upstairs and quickly explained everything to my wife. Five minutes later Mr Hatherley and I were in a cab on our way to Baker Street.

As I had expected, Sherlock Holmes was in his sitting room, reading the small personal advertisements in *The Times* and smoking his pipe. For this early-morning smoke he used all the half-smoked lumps of tobacco from the day before, all carefully dried and collected together. He welcomed us in his usual quiet, pleasant way, and ordered extra food for us. Then we all sat round the table and had a good breakfast. When we had finished, Holmes made Mr Hatherley lie down on the sofa with a glass of brandy and water within reach.

"It is easy to see that your experience has been an extra-ordinary and terrible one, Mr Hatherley," he said. "Please lie down there and make yourself absolutely at home. Tell us what you can, but stop and have a drink when you are tired."

"Thank you," said my patient, "but I have been feeling quite fresh since the doctor bandaged me, and I think that your excellent breakfast has completed the cure. So I will begin the story of my strange experiences at once."

Holmes sat down in his big armchair. As usual, the sleepy expression on his face, and his half-closed eyes, hid his eager-ness. I sat opposite him, and we listened in silence to the strange story our visitor told.

"My parents are dead," he said, "and I am unmarried. I live alone in lodgings in London. By profession I am a hydraulic engineer, and have had seven years of training with Venner and Matheson, the well-known hydraulic engineers, of Green-wich. I completed my training two years ago. Not long before, my father had died and I received some of his money. So I decided to go into business independently, and took an office in Victoria Street.

"The first few years of independent practice are often disappointing. I myself have had an extremely disappointing start. In two years I have had only three or four clients and have earned only twenty-seven pounds. Every day, from nine o'clock in the morning until four in the afternoon, I waited in my little office, until at last I began to lose heart. I thought that I would never get any work.

"Yesterday, however, just as I was thinking of leaving the office, my clerk came in to say that a gentleman was waiting to see me on business. He brought in a card, too, with the name 'Captain Lysander Stark' printed on it. The Captain followed him into the room almost at once. He was a tall, thin man. I do not think I have ever seen a thinner man than Captain Stark. He had a sharp nose and the skin of his face was drawn very tight over the bones. And yet his thinness did not seem to be the result of any disease. His back was straight and his eyes were bright. He was plainly but neatly dressed, and seemed to be about thirty-five or forty years old.

"'Mr Hatherley?' he said, and I thought he sounded like a German. 'You have been recommended to me, Mr Hatherley, not only as an excellent engineer, but also as a man who can keep a secret.'

"This polite remark pleased me. I bowed. 'May I ask who it was who spoke so favourably of me?' I said.

"'Well, perhaps I had better not tell you that just now. I have also heard that your parents are dead, and that you are unmarried and live alone in London.'

"'That is quite correct,' I answered. 'But I do not see what connection these things have with my professional ability. My clerk told me that you wished to speak to me about a professional matter.'

"'Yes, certainly. But everything I have said is important. I have work for you, but absolute secrecy is quite essential — *absolute* secrecy. And of course we can expect greater secrecy from a man who is alone in the world than from one who lives with his family.'

"'If I promise to keep a secret,' I said, 'you can trust me to do so.'

"He looked at me with great suspicion as I spoke. 'You do

promise, then?' he said at last.

"'Yes, I promise.'

"'You promise absolute and complete silence, both before and after doing the work? You promise not to mention the matter at all, either in speech or in writing?'

"'I have already given you my word.'

"'Very good!' He suddenly sprang up, rushed across the room, and threw open the door. The passage outside was empty.

"'That's all right,' he said, coming back. 'I know that clerks are sometimes eager to know about their masters' affairs. Now we can talk in safety.' He drew up his chair very close to mine, and once again began looking suspiciously and thoughtfully at me.

"I did not like this. I was beginning to feel impatient with my strange client.

"'Please tell me why you have come to see me, sir.' I said. 'My time is of value.' Of course this was not really true!

"'Would fifty pounds for a night's work suit you?' he asked.

"'Yes, very well indeed!'

"'I said a *night's* work, but in fact the work would hardly take an hour. I only want your opinion about a hydraulic press which is not working properly. If you show us what is wrong we shall soon be able to put it right ourselves. Are you willing to do it?'

"'Yes, I am,' I said. 'The work appears to be light and the pay extremely generous.'

"'Yes. We want you to come tonight, by the last train.'

"'Where to?' I asked.

"'To Eyford, in Berkshire. It is a little village about seven miles from Reading. There is a train from Paddington which would bring you there at about a quarter past eleven.'

"'Very good.'

"'I will come to Eyford Station in a carriage to meet you.'

"'Do you live far from the station, then?' I asked.

"'Yes, our house is quite out in the country — more than seven miles away.'

"'Then we shall not reach your house before midnight. I

suppose there are no trains back from Eyford to London in the middle of the night. I should have to sleep at your house.'

"'Oh yes, we can easily give you a bed.'

"'That is not very convenient. Couldn't I come at some other time?'

"'We have decided that the night is the best time. The unusually high pay will be your reward for the inconvenience. But of course you are perfectly free to refuse the work if you wish.'

"I thought of the fifty pounds — I thought how very useful the money would be to me. 'I do not want to refuse,' I said. 'I will do whatever you want. But I should like to understand a little more clearly what it is you wish me to do.'

"'Of course. I will explain everything to you. But it is very secret. Are you quite sure that nobody can hear what we are saying?'

"'*Quite* sure,' I replied.

"'Then I will explain. A few years ago I bought a house and a small piece of land, about ten miles from Reading. I discovered that the soil in one of my fields contained fuller's earth. Fuller's earth, as you probably know, is a valuable substance, and is only found in one or two places in England. Unfortunately, however, the amount of fuller's earth in my field was rather small. But to the right and left of it, in fields belonging to my neighbours, there were much larger quantities of the substance. My neighbours had no idea that their land was as valuable as a gold mine. Naturally it was in my interest to buy their land before they discovered its true value; but unfortunately I had no capital with which to do this. I told the secret to a few of my friends, however, and they suggested that we should quietly and secretly dig out our own small quantity of fuller's earth; and that in this way we should earn enough money to buy the neighbouring fields. We have been working secretly like this for some time. One of the machines we use is a hydraulic press. This press, as I have already explained, is not working properly, and we want your advice on the subject. We guard our secret very carefully, however, and if our neighbours found out that a hydraulic engineer had visited our little house, our discovery about the fuller's earth would not be a secret any longer and we should have no chance at all of buying those fields and carrying out our plans. That is why I have made you promise me that you will not tell a single human being that you are going to Eyford tonight. Do you understand?'

"'Yes,' I answered. 'But one point that I do not quite understand is this: how can a hydraulic press be of any use to you in digging fuller's earth out of the ground?'

"'Ah!' he said carelessly, 'we have our own special way. We use the hydraulic press to turn the fuller's earth into bricks — so that we can remove the substance without letting the neighbours know what it is. But that is just a detail. I have taken you into my confidence now, Mr Hatherley, and have shown you that I trust you.' He rose as he spoke. 'I shall expect you, then, at Eyford at eleven fifteen.'

"'I will certainly be there.'

"'And do not say a word about it to anybody!' He gave me a last long, questioning look, and then, pressing my hand in his own cold, damp one, he hurried from the room.

"Well, gentlemen, when I was alone again, I felt very much astonished at this visitor and his unusual request. Of course I was glad in a way, because the money was at least ten times as much as the ordinary pay for such a piece of work. And it was possible that this opportunity would lead to others. However, the face and manner of my new client had given me a feeling of disgust, and I did not believe that the story of the fuller's earth really explained the necessity for a midnight visit, or the conditions of extreme secrecy that were connected with it. But I managed to forget my fears, ate a large supper, drove to Paddington, and started off for Eyford. I had obeyed all Captain Stark's instructions as to holding my tongue.

"At Reading I had to change stations, and caught the last train to Eyford. I reached the dark little station after eleven o'clock. I was the only passenger who got out there, and the only person at the station was a single sleepy railwayman, holding an oil lamp. As I passed through the little gate of the station, however, I found Captain Stark waiting in the shadows on the other side of the road. Without speaking he seized me by the arm and hurried me into a carriage. He pulled up the windows on both sides, knocked on the woodwork as a signal to the driver, and we set off as fast as the horse could go."

"One horse?" Holmes interrupted.

"Yes, only one."

"Did you notice what colour it was?"

"Yes, I saw by the light of the carriage lamps as I was stepping in. It was light brown."

"Was it tired-looking, or fresh?"

"Oh, its coat looked quite fresh."

"Thank you. I am sorry to have interrupted you. Please continue your very interesting statement."

"We drove for at least an hour. Captain Stark had said that it was only about seven miles, but the time the journey took and the speed at which we travelled made me think it was really ten or twelve. He sat at my side in silence, looking hard at me all the time. The country roads must have been rather bad, as the carriage shook and moved violently up and down as we went along. I tried to look out of the windows to see where we were, but they were made of painted glass and I could see nothing except occasional faint lights. Now and then I spoke to the Captain but he answered only 'Yes' or 'No' and the conversation went no further. At last, however, the shaking of the carriage stopped, and we drove over a smooth private road: our journey was over. Captain Stark sprang out, and, as I followed, pulled me quickly through the open front door of the house. We stepped right out of the carriage into the hall, so that I was quite unable to get any idea of what the outside of the house looked like. As soon as I was inside the house the door was shut violently behind us, and I heard the faint sound of wheels as the carriage drove away.

"It was completely dark inside the house, and the Captain began looking for matches, talking to himself as he did so. Suddenly a door opened at the other end of the passage, and a golden line of light appeared. It grew broader, and I saw a woman with a lamp, which she held above her head, pushing her face forward to look at us. I could see that she was pretty, and richly dressed. She said a few words, as though asking a question, in a foreign language, and when my companion answered with a single cold word his reply gave her such a shock that she nearly dropped the lamp. Captain Stark went up to her, whispered something in her ear, and pushed her back into the room she had come out of. Then he walked back towards me with the lamp in his hand, and opened the door of another room.

"'Please be kind enough to wait in this room for a few minutes,' he said.

"It was a small, plainly-furnished room, with a round table in the centre. There were several German books scattered on this table. The Captain put the lamp down on a smaller table by the door. 'I will not keep you waiting long,' he said, and disappeared into the darkness.

"I looked at the books on the table, and although I do not understand German I could see that two of them were on scientific subjects. The others were books of poetry. Then I walked across the window, hoping to see a little of the surroundings of the house. But strong heavy boards were fastened across the window on the outside. It was an extraordinarily silent house. The only sound came from an old clock somewhere in the passage. I felt myself becoming more and more anxious. Who were these German people, and what were they doing, living in this strange, out-of-the-way place? And where *was* the place? I only knew that it was ten or twelve miles from Eyford, but I had no idea whether it was north, south, east, or west. Of course Reading, and possibly other large towns, were about the same distance away. Yet the complete stillness made it clear that Captain Stark's house was right out in the country. I walked anxiously up and down the room, singing to myself under my breath to give myself courage, and feeling that I was thoroughly earning my fifty pounds!

"Then, without a sound, the door of the room swung slowly open, and I saw the woman standing there. Behind her was the darkness of the hall, and the yellow light from my lamp shone on her eager and beautiful face. It was easy to see that she was in a state of extreme fear, and my own blood seemed to turn to ice at the sight. She held up one shaking finger to warn me to be silent. Her eyes, as she looked back into the dark passage, were like those of a frightened horse.

"'You must go away!' she whispered, with an effort to speak calmly. 'There is no good here for you to do.'

"'But I have not yet done what I came to do. I cannot possibly leave until I have seen the machine.'

"'You will gain nothing by staying,' she went on. 'You can pass through the door; nobody can prevent you.' And then, seeing that I only smiled and shook my head, she suddenly gave up her attempt to speak calmly, and took a step forward. 'For the love of heaven!' she said, stretching out her hands towards me, 'get away from here before it is too late!'

"But it is not easy to make me change my mind, and difficulties merely encourage me in the course I have chosen. I thought of my fifty pounds, of the tiring journey I had just made, and of the unpleasant night that was just beginning. Must all this be completely wasted? Why should I run away without carrying out my client's orders, and without receiving my pay for the night's work? It was possible that this woman was mad! Though her warning had worried me, I still shook my head firmly, and said I would stay. She would have gone on trying to persuade me, but just then we heard the noisy closing of a door upstairs, and the sound of footsteps on the stairs. She listened for an instant, threw up her hands in despair, and then disappeared as suddenly and silently as she had come.

"When Captain Stark came back into the room there was

another man with him. This second man was short and fat, with a beard like a goat's growing out of the folds of his round face. The Captain introduced him to me as Mr Ferguson.

"'Mr Ferguson is my secretary and manager,' said the Captain. Then he gave me a suspicious look and said: 'Mr Hatherley, I had the idea that I left this door shut just now.'

"'Yes,' I replied, 'but the room seemed a little close, and so I opened the door to let some air in.'

"'Well, perhaps we had better begin our business now. Mr Ferguson and I will take you up to see the machine.'

"'I had better put my hat on, I suppose,' I said.

"'Oh no, it is in the house.'

"'What! Do you dig fuller's earth in the house?'

"'No, no. This is only where we press it into bricks. But never mind that! All we wish you to do is to examine the machine and to let us know what is wrong with it.'

"We went upstairs together, the Captain first with the lamp, the fat manager and myself behind him. It was the kind of old house in which it would be easy to get lost — full of passages, narrow winding staircases, and little low doors. There were no floor coverings, and above the ground floor there seemed to be no furniture at all. The plaster was coming off the walls, and the damp was breaking through in ugly green stains. I tried to appear calm and cheerful, but I had not forgotten the warnings of the lady, and watched my two companions anxiously. Ferguson appeared to be a bad-tempered and silent man, but I could tell from his voice that he was at least a fellow-Englishman.

"At last Captain Stark stopped outside a low door, which he unlocked. The room inside was small and square — so small, in fact, that the three of us could hardly have gone inside at the same time. Ferguson remained outside, and I went in with the Captain.

"'We are now,' he said, 'actually inside the hydraulic press, and it would be extremely unpleasant for us if anyone turned it on. The ceiling of this little room is really the moving part of the press, and it comes down with very great force on this metal floor. The machine still works, but there is some stiffness in it and it has lost some of its power. I should like you to examine it, please, and to show us how we can put it right.'

"I took the lamp from him, and examined the machine very thoroughly. It was certainly a very large and powerful one. When I went back outside, however, and pressed down the handles that controlled it, I could tell from the soft whistling sound that there was a slight escape of water from one part into another. This was the explanation of the loss of pressure. A further examination showed that one of the rubber bands in the press had become worn and thin, and was the cause of the escape of water. I pointed this out to my companions, who listened very carefully to what I said, and asked several practical questions as to what they should do to put the trouble right. When I had made it clear to them, I went back inside the machine, and had another good look at it — to satisfy my own desire to find out what it was. I realised that the story of the fuller's earth was a complete lie: it was impossible to believe that such a powerful machine could be intended for such a purpose. The walls were made of wood, but the floor was like a kind of iron bath. When I examined this more closely I saw that it was coated with another sort of metal, ground down to powder. I had bent down and was scraping at this to find out exactly what it was, when I heard a few angry words in German and saw the Captain looking down at me.

"'What are you doing in there?' he asked.

"I was feeling angry with him for telling me lies. 'I was admiring your fuller's earth,' I said. 'I think you ought to have told me the real purpose of your machine before asking me to advise you about it.'

As soon as I had spoken I regretted what I had said. A cold, hard expression came into Captain Stark's face, and I saw that his grey eyes were full of hatred.

"'Very well!' he said. 'I will show you *everything* about the machine!' He took a step backwards, shut the little door and quickly turned the key. I rushed towards it and pulled at the handle. Then I pushed and kicked at the door, but it held firm. 'Captain Stark! Captain Stark!' I shouted. 'Let me out!'

"And then suddenly in the silence I heard a sound that seemed to send my heart to my mouth with fear. It was the controlling handles being pressed down, and the slight whistling noise of the water. Captain Stark had turned on the machine. The lamp was still on the iron floor of the press, and by its light I saw that the black ceiling was coming down upon me — slowly and unsteadily, but with enough power to grind and crush me into the floor. With a terrible cry I threw myself against the door, and dragged with my nails at the lock. I begged the Captain to let me out, but the sounds of the machinery drowned my cries. The ceiling was now only a foot or two above my head, and by raising my arm I could feel its hard rough surface. Then the thought struck me that the pain of my death would depend very much upon the position of my body at the last moment. If I lay on my face the weight would come on my backbone, and I trembled to think of the terrible sound of my own back breaking. Perhaps it would be easier the other way — yet had I enough courage to lie and look up at that fearful black shadow as it came nearer and nearer? Already I was unable to stand up, when I noticed something that brought hope back to my heart.

"I have said that though the floor and the ceiling were made of iron, the walls of the press were wooden. As I gave a last despairing look around, I saw a thin line of yellow light between two of the boards; and this light became broader and broader as a small door was pushed backwards. For an instant I could hardly believe that here indeed was a door that led away from death. The next instant I threw myself through, and lay half fainting upon the other side. The door had closed again behind me, but the crash of the lamp as the ceiling struck it, and a few moments afterwards the sound of the top and bottom of the press meeting, made me realise what a narrow escape I had had.

"Suddenly, as I lay outside the press, I felt somebody pulling at my wrist, and I saw that I was on the stone floor of a narrow passage, and a woman with an oil lamp in her hand was bending over me. It was the same good friend whose earlier warning I had so foolishly failed to take seriously.

"'Come! Come!' she cried. 'They will be here in a moment. They will see that you are not there. Oh, do not waste the precious time, but come with me!'

"This time, at least, I took her advice. Unsteadily, I stood up, and ran with her along the passage and down a winding staircase. This led to another broad passage, and, just as we reached it, we heard the sound of running feet and the shouting of two voices — one answering the other — from the floor where we were, and from the one below. My guide stopped and looked about her as if she did not know what to do. Then she threw open a door which led into a bedroom, through the window of which the moon was shining brightly.

"'It is your only chance,' she said. 'The window is high up, but perhaps you can jump out.'

"As she spoke a light appeared at the other end of the passage, and I saw the thin figure of Captain Stark rushing forward with a lamp in one hand, and a weapon — a kind of meat axe — in the other. I rushed across the bedroom, threw open the window, and looked out. How quiet and pleasant the garden looked in the moonlight! It was about thirty feet down. I climbed out, but hesitated to jump, as I wished to hear what was about to happen between Stark and the lady who had saved me from death. If it were necessary I was determined at any risk to return and help her. This thought had hardly flashed through my mind before he was at the door, pushing his way past her; but she threw her arms around him, and tried to hold him back.

"'Fritz! Fritz! Remember your promise after the last time!' she cried in English. 'You said it would never happen again. He will hold his tongue! Oh, he will hold his tongue!'

"'You are mad, Elise!' he shouted, struggling to break

away from her. 'You will be the ruin of us. He has seen too much. Let me pass, I say!' He pushed her to one side, rushed to the window, and struck at me with his heavy weapon. At that moment I was hanging by my hands to the window sill. I was conscious of a dull pain, and the blow made me let go. I fell into the garden below.

"I was not much hurt by the fall; so I got to my feet and rushed off among the bushes as fast as I could run — I knew that I was not out of danger yet. Suddenly, however, as I ran, I began to feel sick and faint. I looked down at my hand, which by now was really painful, and saw for the first time that my thumb had been cut off, and that blood was pouring from the wound. I attempted to tie my handkerchief round it, but suddenly I seemed to hear a strange singing noise in my ears, and the next moment I fainted and fell.

"I do not know how long I remained unconscious. It must have been a very long time, as it was daybreak when I woke up. My clothes were wet through, and my coat was covered in blood from my wounded hand. The pain reminded me of all the details of my midnight adventure, and I sprang to my feet with the feeling that even now I might not be safe from my enemies. But, to my astonishment, when I looked about me I could see neither the house nor the garden. I had been lying almost at the side of a country road, and not far off I saw a long low building. I walked along towards this, and found that it was the railway station where I had arrived the night before! Except for the wound on my hand, everything that had happened during those terrible hours might have been a dream.

"Still in a half-fainting condition, I went into the station, and asked about the morning train. There would be one to Reading in less than an hour. The same railwayman was on duty as at the time of my arrival. I asked him whether he had ever heard of Captain Lysander Stark. The name was strange to him. Had he noticed a carriage waiting for me the night before? No, he had not. Was there a police station anywhere near? There was one two or three miles away.

"It was too far for me to go, in my weak state. I decided to wait until I got back to London before telling my story to the police. It was about half past six when I arrived, and I went first to have my wound bandaged. After that, the doctor very kindly brought me along here. I should like to put the case into your hands, and will do exactly what you advise."

Sherlock Holmes and I sat in silence for some moments after listening to this extraordinary account. Then Holmes pulled down from a shelf one of the thick, heavy books in which it was his habit to stick pieces from the newspapers.

"Here is an advertisement that will interest you," he said. "It appeared in all the papers about a year ago. Listen to this: — 'Lost on the 9th of this month, Mr Jeremiah Hayling, 26 years old, a hydraulic engineer. He left his lodgings at ten o'clock at night, and has not been heard of since. He was dressed in —' and so on. Yes! That must have been the last time the Captain needed to have his hydraulic press repaired, I think."

"Good heavens!" cried my patient. "Then that explains what the woman said."

"I have no doubt of it," said Holmes. "It is quite clear that the Captain is a determined and pitiless man, who would not allow anything or anybody to stand in his way. Well, every moment is precious, and so, if you feel strong enough, Mr Hatherley, we will go to Scotland Yard and then to Eyford."

Two hours later we were all in the train together, on our way from Reading to the little Berkshire village. There were Sherlock Holmes, the hydraulic engineer, Bradstreet the Scotland Yard detective, another policeman, and myself. Bradstreet had spread a large-scale map of the Eyford district out on the seat, and was drawing a circle with Eyford for its centre.

"There!" he said. "That circle is twenty miles across — ten miles from Eyford in every direction. The place we want must be somewhere near that line. You said ten miles, I think, sir?"

"The drive took more than an hour," said Mr Hatherley.

"And you think that they brought you back all that way while you were unconscious?"

"They must have done so. I have a confused memory, too, of having been lifted and carried somewhere."

"I can't understand why they didn't kill you when they found you in the garden," I said. "Perhaps the woman begged Stark to let you go, and succeeded in softening his cruelty."

"I don't think that very probable," Hatherley answered, "I never saw a more pitiless face than his in my life."

"Oh, we shall soon find an explanation for all that," said Bradstreet. "Well, I have drawn my circle, but I wish I knew at which point upon it the wanted men are to be found."

"I think I could put my finger on the right point," said Holmes quietly.

"Really?" cried Bradstreet. "So you have formed your opinion? Well, then, we shall see who agrees with you. I say it is to the south, as there are very few houses in that direction."

"And I say east," said my patient.

"I think it is to the west," said the second policeman. "There are several quiet little villages up there."

"And I think it is to the north," I said, "because there are no hills there, and Mr Hatherley says that he did not notice the carriage going up any."

Bradstreet laughed. "So we have opinions for north, south, east, and west. Which do you agree with, Mr Holmes?"

"I don't agree with any of them," Holmes answered.

"But we can't *all* be wrong!"

"Oh, yes, you can! This is *my* point," he said, placing his finger on the centre of the circle. "This is where we shall find them."

"But how do you explain the ten-mile drive?" asked Hatherley in surprise.

"Five miles out and five back. Nothing could be simpler. You said yourself that the horse was quite fresh when you got in. That would be completely impossible if the horse had just gone ten miles over rough roads."

"Yes," said Bradstreet thoughtfully. "It's quite a likely explanation. Of course it is not difficult to guess what kind of men these are."

"Yes," said Holmes. "They are forgers of coins on a large scale. The hydraulic press is used to form the mixture of metals with which they imitate silver."

"We have known for some time that a clever group was at work," said Bradstreet. "They have made many thousands of false silver coins. We even had clues which led to Reading. But we could get no further — they had covered their tracks too cleverly. But now I think they are about to fall into our hands."

But Bradstreet was mistaken. Those criminals never fell into the hands of the police. As our train came into Eyford Station we saw a broad line of smoke rising into the air behind some trees in the neighbourhood of the village, and hanging like black feathers high up in the sky.

"Is there a house on fire?" Bradstreet asked as soon as we had got out.

"Yes, sir," said the stationmaster.

"When did the fire break out?"

"I hear that it was during the night, sir, but it has got worse, and by now the house is almost completely destroyed."

"Whose house is it?"

"Doctor Becher's."

"Tell me," Hatherley interrupted, "is Doctor Becher a German, very thin, with a long sharp nose?"

The stationmaster laughed heartily. "No, sir, Doctor Becher is an Englishman, and he's the fattest man in the village. But he has a gentleman staying with him — one of his patients, I believe — who is a foreigner, and *he* is extremely thin."

The stationmaster had not finished speaking before we were all hurrying in the direction of the fire. In front of us on a low hill there was a large white house. Smoke and flames were coming out of every window, while in the garden in front three fire engines were attempting, in vain, to control the fire.

"That's the house!" cried Hatherley in great excitement. "There are the bushes were I lay, and that second window is the one that I jumped from."

"Well, at least," said Holmes, "you have had your revenge upon them. I have no doubt that it was your oil lamp which, when it was crushed in the press, set fire to the wooden walls — though no doubt Stark and Ferguson were too excited by their hunt for you to notice it at the time. Now keep your eyes open in this crowd for those two men — though I fear that by now they are almost at the other end of England."

And Holmes was right in his guess. From that day to this nothing has ever been heard of the beautiful woman, the merciless German, or the bad-tempered, silent Englishman. Early that morning a farmer had met a cart, containing several people and some very large boxes. They were driving fast in the direction of Reading. But the criminals left no further signs and even Holmes failed to discover any clues.

We learnt that the firemen had found a human thumb, recently cut off, on a window sill on the second floor of the house. At about sunset they succeeded in putting the fire out, but by that time the roof had fallen in, and almost nothing remained of the forgers' machinery inside the house. Large masses of tin and other metals were found in a building behind the house, but it was clear that the criminals had taken their stores of false coins away with them in the boxes.

The mystery of how Mr Hatherley had been carried from the garden to the roadside was quickly solved when Holmes found a double line of footprints in the soft earth. The engineer had been carried out by two people, one of whom had very small feet, and the other unusually large ones. On the whole, it was most probable that the silent Englishman — less adventurous or less cruel than the German Captain — had helped the woman to carry the unconscious man out of the way of danger.

"Well," said Hatherley a little sadly, "it has been a strange affair for me! I have lost my thumb, and I have lost fifty pounds in pay, and what have I gained?"

"You have gained experience," said Holmes, laughing. "And you have now got a true and interesting story of your own, which you will be able to tell every day for the rest of your life!"

# The Resident Patient

One October evening Sherlock Holmes and I were returning to our rooms in Baker Street after a long walk. I had been sharing these lodgings with Holmes since the death of my wife in 1894. It was quite late in the evening, but we saw a carriage waiting outside the house.

There was a gentleman waiting for us in our sitting room. He stood up when we came in. He was about thirty-three or thirty-four years old, had thin, artistic hands, and looked unhealthy and tired. He was dressed entirely in black.

"Good evening," said Holmes to him cheerfully. "Please sit down again! What can I do to help you?"

"My name is Doctor Percy Trevelyan," said our visitor, "and I live at 403 Brook Street."

"You have written a book on catalepsy, haven't you?" I asked.

Doctor Trevelyan was very pleased and proud that I knew his book. His pale face became quite red.

"I thought that the book had been completely forgotten!" he said. "Very few copies were sold. I suppose you are a doctor yourself, sir?"

"I used to be an army doctor," I replied, "and after that I was in private practice for a few years."

"My own special interest has always been catalepsy," he said. "I would like to work only on that disease. But one must take what one can get! However, I must not talk too much about my own interests! I realise that your time is valuable, Mr Holmes. Well, some very strange things have been happening recently at the house in Brook Street. And tonight something new has happened. I felt that I *must* come and ask for your advice and your help."

Sherlock Holmes sat down and lit his pipe. "You are welcome!"

he said. "Please give me a complete account of the things that are worrying you. Tell me all the details."

"Some of them are very small and unimportant," said Doctor Trevelyan. "But the affair is so difficult to understand that I will tell you the whole story."

"I am a London University man. I won several prizes at the University. My teachers thought that I would become a very successful doctor. I continued my studies afterwards, worked at King's College Hospital, and wrote my book on catalepsy. But, gentlemen, I had no money. A man who wants to become a specialist must live in the expensive area round Cavendish Square. There are only about twelve possible streets. And the rents are extremely high! One also has to hire a horse and carriage, and buy furniture for one's house. I would have needed ten years to be able to save the necessary money. But suddenly I had a great surprise.

"A stranger came to see me one day in my room at King's College Hospital. This gentleman's name was Blessington.

"'Are you the man who has won so many prizes?' he asked.

"'Yes, I am,' I said, bowing.

"'I want to ask you some questions,' he said. 'First of all, have you any bad habits? Do you drink too much?'

"'Really, sir!' I cried. He was not very polite!

"'Please don't be angry,' he said. 'I had to ask you that question. Why are you not working as a private specialist? I suppose you haven't enough money? I will help you! I will rent a house for you in Brook Street.'

"I was very surprised.

"'Oh, I'm making you this offer for my own sake, not for yours!' he said. 'I will tell you the truth. I have a few thousand pounds that I am not using. I want to spend this money on *you*.'

"'But why?' I asked him.

"'Because I want my money to grow!' he replied.

"'What must I do for you?' I asked.

"'I want you to work as a doctor — as a brain specialist,' he said. '*I* will buy the furniture for your house, pay the rent, and pay all your expenses each week. You can keep a quarter of the money you earn. You will give me the other three-quarters.'

"It was a strange offer, Mr Holmes, but I accepted it. A few weeks later I moved into the house in Brook Street. Mr Blessington came to live there too. He said that his heart was weak: he needed to live near a doctor. He turned the best two rooms into a bedroom and a sitting room for himself. He had strange habits. He seemed to have no friends, and very seldom went out. Regularly every evening, he came into my office to find out how much I had earned. He then took all the money and gave me back exactly a quarter of it. Then he took the rest of the money to the strong box in his bedroom.

"I have been very successful as a specialist, Mr Holmes, and in the last year or two I have made him a rich man.

"A few weeks ago Mr Blessington came down to speak to me. He mentioned a recent London robbery. He seemed to be surprisingly worried and excited, and he wanted workmen to come and put stronger locks on our doors and windows.

"He remained in this strange state of excitement for a week. He never stopped looking anxiously out of the window and did not go out at all. He seemed to be living in terrible fear of something or of somebody, but when I asked him about this he answered me very rudely. Gradually, however, he seemed to forget his fears.

"Then there was an event in our house which brought all his fears back. Two days ago I received a letter, which I will read to you. There is no address or date on it.

Dear Doctor Trevelyan,

I am a Russian nobleman, but I now live in England. For some years I have been suffering from catalepsy. As you are a great and well-known brain specialist, I would like to see you.

I will call on you at about a quarter past six tomorrow evening.

"Of course I was waiting in my office at that time the following evening.

"The Russian was a thin old man who did not look very much like a nobleman. There was a young man with him. He was tall and good-looking, with a dark, fierce face and very powerful arms and chest. He gently supported the old man with a hand under his arm as they entered. Then he helped him to sit down.

"'Please forgive me for coming in with my father, doctor,' said this young man. His voice was that of a foreigner.

"'That is quite all right,' I replied. 'Would you like to stay with your father while I examine him?'

"'No, thank you,' he answered. 'I will go back into the waiting room.'

"Then the young man went out, and I turned to the older man to begin discussing his illness. He was a little stupid, and also he did not speak English very well — so it was difficult.

"Suddenly, however, he stopped answering my questions. I saw that he was sitting very stiffly, and staring at me with strange, empty eyes. He was in a state of catalepsy. Of course I was excited. I examined him very carefully, and took notes of his condition. He seemed to be in exactly the same state as other people who have the illness.

"I decided to give him some treatment. My idea was to make him breathe a medicine called nitrite of amyl. The bottle was in my store room, which is behind the office. So I went out to get it. Unluckily it took me five minutes to find the bottle. Then I went back into my office. Mr Holmes, the old man was not there!

"The waiting room was empty too. The servants had heard nothing. Mr Blessington, who had been out for a short walk, came in soon afterwards. But I did not tell him about the strange disappearance of my Russian clients.

"Well, I did not think the Russians would ever come back. However, this evening, again at a quarter past six, they both came into my office.

"'I am very sorry that I left so suddenly yesterday, doctor,' said the old man.

"'I was certainly surprised!' I replied.

"'I can explain it,' he said. 'When my catalepsy goes away, my mind is always empty. I do not remember what has been happening. Yesterday I woke up in a strange room. I did not know where I was. So I simply walked out into the street.'

"'And when I saw my father come out of your office,' said the son. 'I thought that the examination was over. I did not realise what had really happened until we had reached home.'

"'Well,' I said, laughing, 'I understand everything now.' I turned to the older man. 'I will continue the examination now, sir, if you wish.'

"For about half an hour I discussed the old gentleman's illness with him, and gave him the best advice I could. Then he and his son went away.

"Mr Blessington, who often went for a walk at that time of day, came in soon afterwards and went up to his rooms. A moment later I heard him running down again, and he rushed into my office. He seemed to be almost mad with fear.

"'Who has been in my rooms?' he cried.

"'No one,' I said.

"'That is a lie!' he shouted. 'Come up and look.'

"I went up with him, and he pointed to several footmarks on the pale brown carpet.

"'Those are certainly not the marks of *my* feet!' Mr Blessington said.

"They were indeed much larger, and seemed to be quite new. As you know, it rained hard this afternoon, and the two Russians were my only visitors.

"The younger man must have gone up to Mr Blessington's room. But why? Nothing at all was missing.

"'I was astonished to see that Mr Blessington was crying. He could hardly speak, but he mentioned your name, and of course I came here at once. He will be greatly relieved if you can come back with me now, in my carriage."

Holmes said nothing. He simply gave me my hat, picked up his own, and followed Doctor Trevelyan out of the room.

A quarter of an hour later we arrived at the house in Brook Street. A servant let us in, but suddenly somebody turned off the light in the hall.

We heard the person say in a frightened voice:

"I have a gun! If you come any nearer I will shoot you."

"This is very stupid behaviour, Mr Blessington!" cried the doctor angrily.

"Oh, it is you, Doctor!" said the voice in relief. "But who are these other gentlemen?" He lit the gas light again and examined us carefully. He was a very fat man, but had once been much fatter: the skin hung loosely on his face, which looked very unhealthy. He had thin red hair.

At last he put his gun back into his pocket and said:

"It's all right now. You may come up. I hope I have not annoyed you. — How do you do, Mr Holmes. You must advise me! I suppose that Doctor Trevelyan has told you what has happened?"

"Yes, he has," said Holmes. "Who are these two strangers, Mr Blessington, and why are they your enemies?"

"I don't know, of course!" the fat man answered. "But please come up to my rooms."

We went with him into his bedroom. It was large and comfortably furnished. Pointing to a big black box at the end of the bed, Mr Blessington said:

"I have never been a very rich man, Mr Holmes. But I don't like banks. I don't trust them! All my money is in that box. So of course I am very worried about this affair."

Holmes looked at Blessington in his strange way, and then shook his head.

"I cannot possibly advise you if you try to deceive me," he said.

"But I have told you everything!" said Blessington.

Holmes turned away.

"Good night, Doctor Trevelyan," he said.

"But aren't you going to give me any advice?" cried Blessington in a weak voice.

"My advice to you, sir," Holmes replied, "is to tell the truth."

A minute later we were on our way home. As we walked down Harley Street Holmes said:

"I am sorry we came out so uselessly this evening, Watson. And yet this Brook Street affair is rather interesting."

"I don't understand it at all," I confessed.

"Well, those two men intend to harm Blessington for some reason. The young man went up to Blessington's rooms on both days, I am sure. By chance Blessington was out."

"But Doctor Trevelyan thought the old man really had catalepsy!" I said.

"It is not difficult to imitate catalepsy: I have done it myself."

"Why did the men choose such an unusual time of day?"

"Because there must be nobody else in the waiting room. Watson, it is easy to see that Blessington is frightened for his life. And of course he knows who these two terrible enemies are. Perhaps tomorrow he will stop telling me lies."

Holmes woke me up at half past seven the next morning.

"There is a carriage waiting for us, Watson," he said.

"What is the matter?" I asked him.

"I have had a note from Doctor Trevelyan. In it he says: 'Come at once!' — and nothing else."

Twenty minutes later we were back at the doctor's house. He came running out to meet us. His face was very white.

"Oh, it's terrible!" he cried, putting his hands to his eyes.

"What has happened?" we asked.

"Blessington has killed himself."

Holmes whistled.

"Yes," Doctor Trevelyan continued, "he hanged himself during the night."

We went in with him. He took us into the waiting room.

"The police are already up there," he said. "This death has been a terrible shock to me."

"When was he found?" Holmes asked.

"One of the servants takes him a cup of tea at seven o'clock every morning. When she went into his bedroom this morning she saw the poor man hanging in the middle of the room. He had tied a rope to the hook on which the heavy lamp usually hangs. And he had jumped off from the top of his strong box — which he showed us yesterday!"

After thinking for a moment Holmes said:

"I would like to go up now."

We all went up to Blessington's bedroom.

The body looked hardly human. A police officer was beside it, writing in his notebook.

"Ah, Mr Holmes!" he said. "I am very glad to see you."

"Good morning, Lanner," Holmes said. "Have you heard of all the events of the last few days?"

"Yes."

"And what is your opinion of the affair?"

"I think that fear had made Mr Blessington mad. He went to bed — his bed has been used, as you can see. Then at about five o'clock he got up and hanged himself."

I felt the body.

"Yes, he seems to have been dead for about three hours," I said.

'Have you found anything unusual in the room?" Holmes asked the police officer.

"Well, sir, Mr Blessington seems to have smoked a lot during the night. I found these four cigar ends in the fireplace."

Holmes looked at them.

"And have you found Blessington's cigar holder?"

"No. I haven't seen one."

"And where is his cigar case?"

"Here it is. I found it in his coat pocket."

Holmes opened it and smelt the one cigar which it contained.

"Oh, this is a Cuban cigar," he said. "These others are Dutch." He took out his magnifying glass and examined them. "Two of these were smoked through a cigar holder. The other two were not. Two were cut by a not very sharp knife, and the other two were bitten — by a person with excellent teeth. Mr Blessington did not kill himself. He was murdered."

"That is impossible!" cried Lanner.

"Why?"

"Murderers never hang people! And in any case, how did they get in?"

"Through the front door."

"The bar was across it this morning."

"Because someone inside the house put the bar across. In a moment I will tell you how this murder was done."

He went over to the door and examined the lock. Then he took out the key and examined that too; next he looked at the bed, the floor, the chairs, the dead body, and the rope. At last he told us that he was satisfied, and we cut the rope and laid the body gently on the bed. We covered it with a sheet.

"Where did the rope come from?" Holmes asked.

"It was cut off this longer one," said Doctor Trevelyan. He showed us a rope under the bed. "He was terribly afraid of fire. He always kept this rope near him, so that he could climb down from the window if the stairs were on fire."

"Yes, all the facts are now very clear," Holmes said. "I hope that I shall soon be able to tell you the reasons for them as well. I will borrow this photograph of Blessington, as it may help me in my inquiries."

"But you haven't told us anything!" cried Doctor Trevelyan.

"Oh, there were two murderers — the men who pretended to be Russian noblemen — and they were helped by one of your own servants."

"My man has certainly disappeared," said the doctor.

"He let the murderers into the house," Holmes went on. "Mr Blessington's door was locked, but they turned the key with a strong piece of wire. You can see the scratches, even without the magnifying glass.

"They must have fastened a handkerchief over Mr Blessington's mouth, to prevent him from crying out. Then they held a kind of trial — a trial in which they themselves were the judges. During that trial they smoked cigars.

"When the trial was over they took Blessington and hanged

him. Then they left. The servant put the bar across the front door after they had gone."

Lanner hurried away to try to find the servant. Holmes and I returned to Baker Street for breakfast.

"I shall be back by three o'clock," he said when we had finished our meal. "Lanner and Doctor Trevelyan will meet me here then."

The police officer and the doctor arrived at three, but Holmes did not join us until a quarter to four. I could see, however, that he was cheerful.

"Have you any news, Lanner?" he asked.

"We have caught the servant, sir," Lanner replied.

"Excellent! And I have discovered who the murderers are. Their names are Biddle and Hayward."

"The Worthingdon Bank robbers!" cried Lanner.

"Yes. And the man who used the name 'Blessington' was another of them."

"So his real name must have been Sutton. Everything is clear now!" said Lanner.

But Trevelyan and I still did not understand.

"Have you forgotten the great Worthingdon Bank robbery?" said Holmes. "There were four robbers — Biddle, Hayward, Sutton, and a man called Cartwright. A night watchman was killed, and the thieves got away with seven thousand pounds. That was fifteen years ago. At the trial there was not much proof against the robbers, but this man Blessington (that is, Sutton) decided to help the police. The result was that Cartwright was hanged, and Biddle and Hayward were sent to prison for fifteen years. When they were let out they decided to punish Sutton (that is, Blessington) for what he had done."

Nobody was punished for Blessington's death. Biddle and Hayward were drowned soon afterwards when a steamer called the *Norah Creina* sank off the coast of Portugal. And there was not enough proof against Doctor Trevelyan's man. So he was never tried: and no complete account of the Brook Street mystery has ever been given to the public till now.

# The Disappearance of Lady Frances Carfax

"Turkish, Watson?" asked Sherlock Holmes, looking at my shoes.

"No, they are English, of course!" I answered. "I bought them here in London, at Latimer's in Oxford Street."

Holmes smiled.

"I was not talking about your shoes, Watson," he said. "I was talking about the bath! You have had a Turkish bath today, haven't you?"

"Yes, I have. But how did you know that, Holmes?"

"My dear Watson, I looked at your shoes."

"Perhaps I am a little stupid," I said, "because I don't understand how a pair of English shoes and a Turkish bath can be connected! Won't you explain?"

"It is very simple," he said. "You are in the habit of fastening your shoes in a particular way. But today they are fastened with a beautiful double knot. So it is clear that you have taken them off. And somebody else has fastened them for you. Who was this person? A man in a shoe shop? No. You bought some new shoes only a week ago. It was not a man in a shoe shop. It was the servant at the Turkish bath. It is simple, isn't it? And why, Watson, did you go to the Turkish bath?"

"Because I have been feeling old and ill for the last few days. A Turkish bath usually makes me feel well again."

"You need a change, Watson. I suggest Switzerland. Would you like to stay at the best hotel in Lausanne? You would live like a king, and it would be completely free! And of course you would travel first class on the train."

"That would be wonderful," I said. "But why are you offering me an opportunity like this?"

Holmes did not answer. Instead, he leaned back in his chair

and took his notebook from his pocket.

"Chickens are helpless among wild animals, Watson," he began at last. "And unmarried ladies who wander about the world from one hotel to another put themselves in great danger from wicked people. If such a lady disappears, nobody misses her. I very much fear that some terrible harm has come to Lady Frances Carfax.

"Lady Frances," he continued, "is the last member of a noble family. Her father and her brothers are all dead. She is not a rich woman, but she has some fine old Spanish jewellery, made of silver and beautiful diamonds. She loves this jewellery so much that she has always refused to leave it at her bank for safety. So she carries her diamonds about with her everywhere. Watson, I am sorry for Lady Frances Carfax. She is not old; she is still a beautiful woman; and yet she is completely alone in the world."

"And what has happened to her?" I asked.

"Ah, Watson, that is the mystery *we* have to deal with! I don't even know whether she is alive or dead. She is a lady of very regular habits, and for the last four years she has written a letter every two weeks to her old nurse. The nurse, whose name is Miss Dobney, lives in Camberwell, here in London. It is Miss Dobney who has asked for my help. Lady Frances has not written to her for nearly five weeks. Her last letter came from the National Hotel in Lausanne. The manager of the hotel says that the lady left without telling anybody her new address. Miss Dobney is very anxious about her. So are Lady Frances's rich and noble cousins. We shall not run short of money, Watson!"

"Is Miss Dobney the only person Lady Frances writes to here in England?"

"No. There is also the manager of her bank. I have talked to him. He showed me her used cheques There were two recent ones. The first was for a very large amount, much more than enough to pay her hotel bill. The second cheque was for fifty pounds, and was made out to Miss Marie Devine. The money was paid to Miss Devine less than three weeks ago, at a bank in Montpellier in the south of France."

"And who is Miss Marie Devine?" I asked.

"I have already found that out," Holmes answered. "She was Lady Frances's servant. I have not yet found out why Lady Frances gave her that cheque. I have no doubt, however, that you will be able to discover the reason."

"*I*, Holmes!"

"Yes, Watson. That was why I suggested a holiday in Switzerland. You know that I cannot possibly leave London just now. The London police would feel lonely if I went abroad! So you must go, Watson. Send me a telegram if you need my advice."

Two days later I was at the National Hotel in Lausanne. The manager, Mr Moser, told me that Lady Frances had stayed there for several weeks. Everyone who met her had liked her very much. She was not more than forty years old. She was still a fine woman, and one could see that she had once been very beautiful. Mr Moser did not know that she had any valuable jewellery. However, the servants had noticed that there was one large heavy box that was always locked. Marie Devine, the maid, was as popular as Lady Frances herself. In fact she was going to marry one of the waiters at the hotel. I had no difficulty in getting her address. It was 11, rue de Trajan — that is, Trajan Street — Montpellier, France. I wrote all this down in a little notebook. I was proud of my cleverness: Holmes himself could not have gathered together more facts!

But the biggest mystery still remained. What was the reason for Lady Frances's sudden decision to leave? She was very happy in Lausanne. Everyone had expected her to stay for several months. She had had lovely rooms with a view of the Lake of Geneva. And yet she had left so suddenly! She had even had to pay a week's rent uselessly! Mr Moser could not understand it. Only Jules Vibart, the waiter who was going to marry Marie Devine, was able to give me any useful information. A day or two before Lady Frances left, a tall, dark man with a beard had visited the hotel.

"He was like a wild animal!" cried Jules Vibart.

The man had rooms somewhere in the town. Vibart and Marie had seen him by the lake with Lady Frances, talking very earnestly to her. The next time the man came to the hotel, Lady Frances had refused to see him. He was English, but Vibart did not know his name. Lady Frances had left Lausanne immediately afterwards. Vibart and Marie both thought that the strange Englishman's visit was the cause of Lady Frances's decision to leave.

I asked Vibart why Marie had left the lady. But he refused to answer.

"I cannot tell you that, sir," he said. "If you want to find out, you must go to Montpellier and ask Marie herself."

After my conversations with Mr Moser and Vibart, I tried to find out where Lady Frances had gone to from Lausanne. I discovered that there had been some secrecy. Perhaps Lady Frances had been trying to escape from someone? Certainly it was strange that her cases and boxes had not been clearly marked. She had reached Baden-Baden in Germany with her luggage after a very long and indirect journey. I found this out from one of the local travel agents.

I therefore bought a ticket to Baden-Baden myself. Before I left Lausanne I sent Holmes a telegram. In it I gave him an account of everything I had done. In his reply he said that he was proud of me. I did not know whether he was joking or serious.

At Baden-Baden I was told that Lady Frances had stayed at the English Hotel for two weeks. At the hotel she had met a man called Doctor Schlessinger and his wife. Doctor Schlessinger was a minister of religion, and he and his wife had worked in South America, where he had fallen ill.

Lady Frances was a very religious woman, and for her it was an honour to know this holy man. She gladly helped Mrs Schlessinger to look after him. He used to sit all day in a chair bed outside the hotel with a lady on each side of him. He was preparing a religious map of Egypt, and was also writing a history book on the same subject.

Finally, when Doctor Schlessinger's health had improved a little, he and his wife had returned to London. Lady Frances had gone with them, and Doctor Schlessinger had paid her hotel bill. It was now three weeks since they had left.

I asked the manager about Marie Devine, Lady Frances's servant.

"She left a few days before the Schlessingers and Lady Frances went to England," he answered. "She was crying very noisily, and she said to me: 'I don't want to be a maid ever again!'"

The manager went on, after a pause:

"You are not the first person who has asked for information about Lady Frances Carfax. About a week ago another Englishman came here to ask questions about her."

"Did he tell you his name?" I asked.

"No. He was a very strange man!"

"Was he like a wild animal?" I was thinking of what Jules Vibart had told me in Lausanne.

"Yes! A wild animal," said the manager. "That is a perfect description of him. He was a large man with a brown face and a beard. He was like a rough, fierce farmer. I would not like to be his enemy!" Already the explanation of the mystery was becoming clear. This evil, cruel man was chasing the poor good lady from place to place. It was clear that she was terribly afraid of him: otherwise she would not have left Lausanne. And now he had followed her as far as Baden-Baden. Sooner or later he would catch up with her! Had he already caught up with her, perhaps? Was *that* the explanation of her disappearance?

I hoped that the good Doctor Schlessinger and his wife would be able to protect her from this wicked man.

In another telegram to Holmes I told him that I had discovered who was to blame in the matter. But instead of a reply I received this:

## DESCRIBE DOCTOR SCHLESSINGER'S LEFT EAR, PLEASE. — HOLMES.

Holmes's little joke did not amuse me. In fact I was rather annoyed.

Next I went to Montpellier to see Marie Devine. She was very helpful. She had loved Lady Frances, she said, but recently Lady Frances had not been kind to her, and had even accused her of stealing.

I asked her about the cheque for fifty pounds.

"It was a present, sir," she replied. "I am going to be married soon."

We then spoke of the strange Englishman.

"Ah, he is a bad man, sir!" said Marie. "A fierce and terrible man. I myself have seen him seize Lady Frances by the wrist, and hurt her. It was by the lake at Lausanne, sir."

Marie was sure that fear of this man was the cause of Lady Frances's sudden journeys. The poor lady was trying to escape from him.

"But look, sir!" Marie suddenly said. "He's out there — the man himself!" She sounded frightened.

I looked out of the window. A very tall, dark man with a large black beard was walking slowly down the centre of the street. He was looking up at the numbers of the houses. It was clear that, like myself, he was looking for Marie. Angrily, I ran out of the house and spoke to him.

"You are an Englishman," I said.

"I don't want to speak to you," he said rudely.

"May I ask what your name is?"

"No, you may not!" he answered.

It was a difficult situation. The only way to deal with it was to use the direct method of shock.

"Where is Lady Frances Carfax?" I asked.

He looked at me in astonishment.

"What have you done with her?" I continued. "Why have you been following her? I want an answer from you at once!"

The man gave a roar of anger and sprang at me. I am not a weak man, but he was as strong as a horse. He fought like a devil, and soon his hands were round my throat. I was nearly unconscious when a French workman rushed out of a little hotel and saved me. He struck the Englishman on the arm with his stick: this made him loosen his hold on my throat. The wild man then stood near us for a moment, unable to decide whether to attack me again. Finally he turned angrily away and went into the house where Marie lived. I began to thank the kind Frenchman beside me.

"Well, Watson," he said, "you haven't done very well this time! I think you had better come back with me to London by the night train."

An hour later Sherlock Holmes, wearing his own clothes now, was with me in my private sitting room at the hotel.

"I did not expect to be able to get away from London," he said, "but here I am after all!"

"And how did you know that I would be here in Montpellier?" I asked him.

"It was easy to guess that Montpellier would be the next stage of your travels," Holmes said. "Since I arrived I have been sitting in that little hotel, waiting for you. And really, Watson, what a situation you have got into!"

"Perhaps you would not have done any better yourself," I answered, annoyed.

"I *have* done better, Watson!"

Just then one of the hotel servants brought somebody's card in. Holmes looked at it.

"Ah, here is Mr Philip Green. Mr Green is staying at this hotel, and he may be able to help us to find out what has happened to Lady Frances Carfax."

The man who came in was the same wild person who had attacked me in the street. He did not look pleased when he saw me.

"I received your letter, Mr Holmes," he said. "But why is this man here? In what way can he be connected with the affair?"

"This is my old friend Doctor Watson," replied Holmes. "He is helping us in this case."

The stranger held out his large brown hand.

"I am very sorry about what happened, Doctor Watson," he said. "When you accused me of hurting Frances I lost all my self-control. I am in a terrible state, you know. I don't understand this affair at all. And, Mr Holmes, I don't even know who told you of my existence!"

"I have spoken to Miss Dobney, Lady Frances's old nurse," Holmes said.

"Old Susan Dobney with the funny hat!" said Green. "I remember her well."

"And she remembers you. She knew you in the days before you went to South Africa."

"Ah, I see that you know my whole story. I will not hide anything from you, Mr Holmes. I have loved Frances all my life. When I was a young man I did some bad things. And she was always so pure and good! So when somebody told her how I was living, she refused to speak to me again. And yet she loved me. She loved me well enough to remain unmarried for my sake. I stayed for many years in South Africa. I made money. When I came back to Europe I decided to find her — to try to persuade her to marry me. I knew that she was still unmarried. I found her in Lausanne. I think I almost persuaded her, but her will was strong. The next time I went to her hotel I was told that she had left the town. I tracked her as far as Baden-Baden, and then after a time I learnt that her servant was here. I am a rough sort of person; I have had a rough sort of life; and when Doctor Watson spoke to me as he did I became quite wild for a moment. But Mr Holmes, tell me what has happened to Lady Frances!"

"We will do our best to find that out," said Holmes in a serious voice. "What is your address in London, Mr Green?"

"You can send letters or messages to the Langham Hotel."

"I think you ought to return to London," Holmes said. "I may need you there. I promise you that everything possible will be done for the safety of Lady Frances Carfax. Meanwhile, here is my card with my address on it. Now, Watson, while you are packing your bag, I will send a telegram to Mrs Hudson. I will ask her to prepare a really good dinner for two hungry travellers at half past seven tomorrow evening."

We found a telegram for Holmes on our table the following evening.

"TORN, NOT REGULAR" was the message, which came from Baden-Baden.

"What does this mean?" I asked.

"It is the answer to a question about Doctor Schlessinger's ear. You may remember my telegram. You did not answer it."

"I thought it was a joke."

"Indeed? Well, I sent the same message to the manager of the English Hotel. This telegram is his answer. An important answer, Watson — very important!"

"What does it prove?"

"It proves, my dear Watson, that we are dealing with a clever and dangerous man. His name is Henry Peters, or 'Holy' Peters, from Adelaide in Australia. He is one of the most evil men in the world, Watson. He is specially skilful at robbing lonely ladies by making use of their religious feelings. He is helped in this by a friend of his, a woman called Annie Fraser, who pretends to be his wife. I suspected that 'Doctor Schlessinger' was really Mr Peters. The matter of the torn ear makes it quite certain."

"And how did 'Holy' Peters get his torn ear?" I asked.

"He was hurt in a fight at an Adelaide hotel," Holmes replied. "It happened about six years ago. Well, Watson, poor Lady Frances is in the hands of a terrible pair. Perhaps she is already dead. Indeed that is quite probable. If she is still alive she is certainly a prisoner somewhere. She is unable to write letters to Miss Dobney or to anybody else. I believe that Lady Frances is here in London. In London it is easy to keep a person a prisoner in complete secrecy. After dinner I will go along to Scotland Yard and speak to our friend Lestrade."

But the police did not manage to discover anything. The three people we wanted to find had completely disappeared. We advertised in the newspapers, but this failed. The police watched all 'Holy' Peters's old friends, but he did not visit them. And then, suddenly, after a week of hopeless waiting, something happened. A piece of old Spanish jewellery, made of silver and diamonds, had been received by a pawnbroker in Westminster Road. The man who brought it in was a large man who looked like a priest. The name and address he gave were clearly false. The pawnbroker had not noticed his ear, but we were sure that this was 'Holy' Peters.

Philip Green had already come to see us twice, anxiously hoping for news. The third time he came, we were able to tell him something at last.

"Peters has taken some of Lady Frances's jewellery to a pawnbroker's shop," Holmes told him. "We are going to catch him now."

"But does this mean that any harm has come to Lady Frances?" asked Green.

Holmes gave him a very serious look.

"If Peters and Annie Fraser have kept her a prisoner until now, they cannot set her free without danger to themselves. I fear the worst, Mr Green."

"Please give me something to do, Mr Holmes!" said Green.

"Do these people know you?" asked Holmes.

"No."

"Peters will probably go back to the same pawnbroker's when he needs money again. I will give you a letter to the pawnbroker, and he will let you wait in the shop. If Peters comes in, you must follow him home. But you must not let him see you. And of course you must not attack him. Please do nothing without telling me."

For two days Green brought us no news. Then, on the evening of the third day, he rushed into our sitting room, pale and trembling with excitement.

"We have caught him!" he cried. "We have caught him!"

He was so excited that he could hardly speak. Holmes pushed him into an armchair.

"Please, Mr Green," he said, "tell us what has happened."

"She came into the shop an hour ago. It was the wife this time, but the piece of jewellery she brought was just like the other. She is a tall, pale woman, with eyes like a rat's."

"That is the woman," said Holmes.

"She left the shop and I followed her. She walked up Kennington Road. Then she went into another shop. Mr Holmes, it was an undertaker's!"

I could see the shock on Holmes's face.

"Go on," he said, forcing himself to speak calmly.

"I went in too," said Green. "She was talking to the undertaker inside. I heard her say: 'It is late.' The undertaker replied: 'It has probably arrived by now. It took longer than an ordinary one would take.' Then they both stopped and looked at me. So I asked the undertaker the way to Waterloo Station and then left the shop."

"You have done well, Mr Green," said Holmes. "Excellently well! And what happened next?"

"The woman came out. I had hidden in the doorway of another shop. I think she was suspicious of me, because I saw her looking all round for me. Then she called a cab and got in. I managed to get another cab and so to follow hers. She got out at 36 Poultney Square, in Brixton. I drove past, left my cab at the corner of the square, and watched the house."

"Did you see anyone?" asked Holmes.

"Only one window was lighted, on the ground floor. I could not see in. I was standing there, wondering what I ought to do next, when a cart stopped outside the house. Two men got out, took something out of the cart, and carried it up the steps to the front door. Mr Holmes, it was a coffin!"

"Ah!"

"For a moment I thought of rushing into the house. The door had been opened to let the men in with the coffin. It was the woman called Fraser who had opened it. But as I stood there she saw me. I think she recognised me. I saw her face change, and she closed the door at once. I remembered my promise to you, and here I am."

"You have done excellent work," said Holmes. He wrote a few words on a half-sheet of paper. "A search warrant is necessary now. Please take this note to Mr Lestrade at Scotland Yard. He will arrange everything. There may be some difficulty, but the affair of the jewellery is good enough proof of some crime, I think."

"Meanwhile Frances may be murdered!" said Green. "That coffin must surely be for her."

"We will do everything that can be done, Mr Green. We are not going to waste any time. Now, Watson," he said, as Green hurried away, "to me the situation seems so terrible that we must act now, without the help of the law. You and I are the unofficial police of London. We must go to Poultney Square immediately."

When we were in the cab, going at high speed over Westminster Bridge, Holmes gave me his views on 'Holy' Peters's plans.

"These wicked people have persuaded this poor lady to dismiss her faithful servant and to come to London with them. If she has written any letters they have been stolen and destroyed. The criminals have rented a furnished house. They have made her a prisoner, and now they have got possession of her jewellery. That jewellery was the original reason for their interest in Lady Frances. Already they have begun to exchange it for money: they do not know that she has friends who are tracking them. They cannot set her free, and they cannot keep her a prisoner for ever. So they must kill her."

"That seems very clear," I said.

"And the arrival of the coffin proves, I fear, that she is already dead. Oh, Watson, there is the undertaker's, I think. Stop, driver! Will you go in, Watson? Ask the undertaker when the Poultney Square funeral is to be."

The man in the shop told me that it was arranged for eight o'clock the next morning.

When I told this to Holmes he looked rather unhappy.

"I can't understand it at all," he said. "Murderers usually bury the body in a hole in the back garden. *These* murderers seem to fear nothing! We must go forward and attack, Watson. Are you armed?"

"I have my stick, at least."

"Well, well, we shall be strong enough. We simply cannot afford to wait for the police or the search warrant. Thank you, driver; you can go."

Holmes rang the bell of a great dark house in the centre of Poultney Square. The door was opened at once by a tall woman.

"Well, what do you want?" she said rudely, looking at us in the darkness.

"I want to speak to Doctor Schlessinger," said Holmes.

"There is no Doctor Schlessinger here," she answered. Then she tried to close the door, but Holmes had put his foot in the way.

"Well, I want to see the man who lives here. I don't care what he calls himself," he said firmly.

She hesitated. Then she pulled the door wide open.

"Well, come in!" she said. "My husband is not afraid to see any man in the world." She closed the door behind us, and took us into a sitting room on the right of the hall. Before she left us she turned up the gas light in the room. "Mr Peters will be with you in a moment," she said.

Almost at once a man came into the dusty sitting room. He made no noise as he walked. 'Holy' Peters was a big man with a large fat red face, who would have looked pleasant if he had not had such a cruel mouth. And he had no hair on his head.

"You have surely made a mistake, gentlemen," he said in an oily voice. "I think you have come to the wrong house. If you tried further down the street, perhaps . . . "

"You are wasting your breath," said my friend. "My name is Sherlock Holmes. You are Henry Peters, of Adelaide, formerly

Doctor Schlessinger of Baden-Baden and South America."

"I am not afraid, Mr Holmes. What is your business in my house?"

"I want to know what you have done with Lady Frances Carfax, who came away with you from Baden-Baden."

"I would be very glad if you could tell me where she is," Peters answered calmly. "She borrowed nearly a hundred pounds from me, and has not paid me. She only gave me some almost valueless jewellery, instead of the money. I paid her hotel bill at Baden-Baden and I bought her a ticket from there to London. We lost her at Victoria Station. If you can find her, Mr Holmes, I shall be very grateful to you."

"I am going to find her," said Sherlock Holmes. "I am going to search this house until I do find her."

"And where is your search warrant?" Peters asked.

Holmes took out a gun from his pocket.

"So you are a common robber!" said Peters.

"That is right. And my friend Watson is also a dangerous man. We are now going to search your house together."

'Holy' Peters opened the door.

"Fetch a policeman, Annie!" he called out.

We heard the woman run across the hall and go out through the front door.

"We have very little time, Watson," said Holmes. "If you try to stop us, Peters, you will certainly get hurt. Where is the coffin that was brought into this house?"

"Why do you want to look at the coffin?" Peters asked. "It is in use. There is a body in it."

"I must see that body."

"I refuse to show it to you!"

But Holmes had pushed him out of the way. We went together into the next room. It was the dining room of the house. The gas light was burning low, but we saw the coffin at once. It was on the table. Holmes turned up the gas and opened the coffin. Deep down at the bottom there was the body of a small, very thin, and very, very old woman. It was certainly not Lady Frances

Carfax.

"Thank God!" whispered Holmes in relief. "It is someone else."

"You have made a bad mistake, haven't you, Mr Holmes?" said Peters, who had followed us into the room.

"Who is this dead woman?" asked Holmes.

"You have no right to ask. But I will tell you. She is my wife's old nurse, Rose Spender. We found her in Brixton Old People's Hospital, and brought her here. We called in Doctor Horsom. Yes, please write down his address in your notebook, Mr Holmes! It is 13 Firbank Street. He looked after her very carefully, but on the third day she died. She was ninety years old. The funeral is to be at eight o'clock tomorrow morning. The undertaker is Mr Stimson, of Kennington Road."

"I am going to search your house," said Holmes.

"I don't think you are," said Peters, who had heard policemen in the hall. "Come in here, please!" he called out to them. "These men are in my house without permission. Help me to put them out."

Holmes took out one of his cards.

"This is my name and address," he said to the policemen, "and this gentleman is my friend Doctor Watson."

"We know you very well, sir," said one of the policemen, "but you can't stay here without a search warrant."

"Of course not. I realise that," said Holmes.

"Take him to the police station!" cried Peters.

"We know where to find this gentleman if he is wanted," said the policeman in reply; "but you must go now, Mr Holmes. That is the law."

We went next to Brixton Old People's Hospital. There we were told that two kind people had claimed a dying woman as a former servant of theirs, and had received permission to take her away with them.

We then went to see Doctor Horsom, who had looked after the old woman before she died.

"I was with her when she died," he told us. "Old age was the cause of death. There was nothing suspicious about the death at all."

"Did you notice anything suspicious in the house?" asked Holmes.

"No. There was only one strange thing. Mr and Mrs Peters had no servants. That was unusual for people of their class."

The doctor was unable to tell us anything more.

Finally we went to Scotland Yard. We were told that the search warrant would probably not be signed until next morning at about nine.

Sherlock Holmes did not go to bed that night. He smoked for hours, and wandered about the house. At twenty past seven in the morning he rushed into my room.

"The funeral is at eight, Watson! It is seven-twenty now. And my thoughts on the Carfax mystery have only just become clear! We must hurry. If we are too late . . . '

In less than five minutes we were in a fast cab. However, it was twenty-five to eight as we went over Westminster Bridge, and ten past eight when we arrived in Poultney Square. But the undertaker's men were also a little late, and we were in time to see them carrying the coffin out of the house. Holmes rushed forward.

"Take that coffin back!" he cried, putting his hand on the chest of the first man to push him back into the hall. "Take it back at once!"

Then Peters appeared behind the coffin. His red face was very angry.

"Mr Holmes, you have no right to give orders here!" he shouted. "Show me your search warrant!"

"The search warrant is on its way," Holmes answered. "This coffin must remain in the house until it comes."

The firmness in Holmes's voice had its effect on the undertaker's men. Peters had suddenly disappeared, and they obeyed these new orders.

They put the coffin back on the dining-room table. In less than a minute we had managed to open it. As we did so, a strong smell of chloroform came out. There was a body in the coffin.

The head was wrapped in bandages, which were still wet with the chloroform. Holmes unfastened them and we saw the face of a handsome woman. At once he lifted the body to a sitting position.

"Is she alive, Watson? Surely we are not too late!"

For half an hour it seemed that we were indeed too late. But in the end our efforts to bring the lady back to life were successful. Her breath returned; her eyes began to open. A cab had just arrived, and Holmes went to the window and looked out.

"Here is Lestrade with his search warrant," he said. "But 'Holy' Peters and Annie Fraser have already escaped. — And here is a man who has a better right to nurse this lady than we have! Good morning, Mr Green. I think Lady Frances should be taken away from here as soon as possible. Meanwhile, the funeral may continue. The poor old woman at the bottom of that coffin can now be buried — alone!"

"I have been very stupid, Watson," said Holmes that evening.

"I knew that I had heard *something* important, but I did not know what it was until seven o'clock this morning. It was something the undertaker said to Annie Fraser. Our friend Green heard him say it. *'It took longer,'* the man said, *'than an ordinary one would take.'* Of course he was talking about the coffin. It was an unusual one. Its measurements were not the ordinary ones. It had been made specially — but why? Why? Then I suddenly remembered the deep sides, and the little thin body at the bottom. Why had such a large coffin been made for such a small body?

"There could be only one explanation. It was to leave room for another body: the body of Lady Frances Carfax."

# The Three Garridebs

The case of the three Garridebs began late in June 1902, soon after the end of the South African War. Sherlock Holmes had just spent several days in bed, as was his habit from time to time, but that morning he came out of his bedroom with a pile of handwritten papers in his hand and a look of amusement in his cool grey eyes.

"My dear Watson, here is a chance for you to make some money," he said. "Have you ever heard the name Garrideb?"

I admitted that I had not.

"Well, if you can find a man called Garrideb, both you and he will be rich."

"How can that be so?" I asked.

"Ah, that's a long story — rather an amusing one, too. Quite extraordinary, in fact. A man is coming to see me about it in a few minutes, so I won't begin the story till he arrives. But, meanwhile, Garrideb is the name we want."

The telephone book was on the table beside me, and I turned over the pages in rather a hopeless hunt for a Garrideb. But to my astonishment there was this strange name in its due place. I gave a cry of delight.

"Here you are, Holmes! Here it is!"

Holmes took the book from my hand.

"'Garrideb, N.,'" he read, "'136 Little Ryder Street.' I am sorry to disappoint you, Watson, but this Garrideb is my client himself. That is the address on his letter. We want another Garrideb to match him."

Just then our housekeeper, Mrs Hudson, came in with a card on a tray. I picked it up and looked at it.

"Why, here *is* another!" I cried. "The first name is different. This is John Garrideb, a lawyer from Kansas in America."

Holmes smiled as he looked at the card. "I am afraid you must make one more effort, Watson," he said. "We already know about this gentleman, though I certainly did not expect to see him here this morning. However, he will be able to tell us a good deal that I want to know."

A moment later he was in the room. Mr John Garrideb was a short, powerful man with a round fresh face. It was easy to believe that he was an American businessman or lawyer. He looked rather childlike, and had a broad, fixed smile on his face. His eyes, however, were surprising. I have seldom seen a pair of human eyes which were brighter, quicker, or sharper. His voice was American, but not very noticeably so.

"Mr Holmes?" he asked, looking at each of us in turn. "Ah, yes! The photographs of you in the newspapers are not unlike you, sir, if I may say so. I believe you have had a letter from another Garrideb — Mr Nathan Garrideb — haven't you?"

"Please sit down," said Sherlock Holmes. "I think we shall have a good deal to discuss." He picked up the pile of papers. "You are, of course, the Mr John Garrideb who is mentioned in these law papers. But surely you have been in England for some time?"

"Why do you say that, Mr Holmes?" A sudden look of suspicion appeared in the man's eyes.

"Because all your clothes are English."

Mr Garrideb laughed uncomfortably. "I've read of your clever tricks as a detective, Mr Holmes, but I never thought I would be the subject of them myself. How do you know my clothes are English?"

"By the shoulders of your coat, the toes of your shoes — how could anyone doubt it?"

"Well, well, I had no idea that I looked so much like an Englishman. But I came to England on business some time ago, and so — as you say — nearly all my clothes were bought in London. But I suppose your time is of value, and am not here to talk about fashions in clothes! Please let us now discuss those papers which you have in your hand."

It was clear that in some way Holmes had annoyed our visitor, who now had a much less friendly expression on his round childlike face.

"Have patience, Mr Garrideb!" said my friend gently. "Doctor Watson could tell you that these little tricks of mine are sometimes very useful in the end, in solving mysteries. But why hasn't Mr Nathan Garrideb come with you?"

"Why did he bring you into the affair at all?" asked our visitor, with sudden anger. "What have you to do with it? Here was a bit of professional business between two gentlemen — and now one of them is employing a private detective! I saw him this morning, and he told me of the stupid thing he had done — and that's why I'm here. But I do feel annoyed about it!"

"Nobody suspects you of anything wrong, Mr Garrideb. Mr Nathan Garrideb is only anxious to gain the success which, I believe, is equally important to both of you. He knew that I had means of getting information, and therefore it was very natural that he should come to me."

The anger gradually disappeared from our visitor's face.

"Well, I'm beginning to understand now," he said. "When I went to see him this morning and he told me he had written to a private detective, I just asked for your address and came along at once. I don't want the police mixed up in a private matter. But if you only help us to find the man, there can be no harm in that."

"Well, that is exactly what I am going to do," said Holmes. "And now, sir, as you are here, you had better give us a clear account of the whole affair. My friend here, Doctor Watson, knows nothing of the details."

Mr Garrideb looked at me, in a not very friendly way.

"Need he know?" he asked.

"We usually work together," said Holmes.

"Well, there's no reason why it should be kept secret. I'll tell you the main facts, then. If you came from Kansas I would not need to explain to you who Alexander Hamilton Garrideb was.

He made his money by buying and selling houses and land, and afterwards he made a second fortune in the Chicago wheat market. Then he spent it in buying more land, along the Arkansas River, west of Fort Dodge — and in the end he owned a piece of land as big as Kent or Sussex here in England. It's sheep-farming land and forest and mining land and land for growing crops on — in fact it's more or less every sort of land that brings dollars to the man that owns it.

"He had no relatives — or, if he had, I never heard of it. But he took a kind of pride in his unusual name. That was what brought us together. I was a lawyer at Topeka, and one day I had a visit from the old man, and he was absolutely delighted to meet another man with his own name. And he was determined to find out if there were any more Garridebs in the world. 'Find me another!' he said. I told him I was a busy man and could not spend my life wandering round the world in search of Garridebs. 'But that is exactly what you are going to do if my plans are put into effect,' he replied. I thought he was joking, but I soon discovered that there was a great deal of serious meaning in his words.

"He died less than a year later, and after his death a will was found. It was the strangest will that had ever been seen in the State of Kansas. His property was divided into three parts, and I was to have one on condition that I found two Garridebs who would share the rest. Each of the three shares is worth five million dollars, but until I have found two other Garridebs none of the money is to be paid out.

"It was such a wonderful chance for me that I simply left my practice as a lawyer and set out to look for Garridebs. There is not a single one in the United States. I searched the whole country very thoroughly, sir, but discovered no Garridebs at all. Then I tried England, where I found the name in the London telephone book. I went to see the gentleman two days ago and explained the whole matter to him. But, like myself, he is alone in the world, with some women relatives, but no men. According to the old man's will, the three Garridebs must all be grown-up men. So you see we still need one more man, and if you can help us to find him we will be very ready to pay your charges."

"Well, Watson," said Holmes, with a smile. "I said this was rather an amusing case, didn't I? Mr Garrideb, I think the first thing you should do is to put a small advertisement in the newspapers."

"I have done that already, Mr Holmes. There were no replies."

"Oh, how disappointing! Well, it is certainly a very interesting little problem. I may look into it for you if I have time. It is interesting, Mr Garrideb, that you should come from Topeka. I had a friend there who used to write to me — he is dead now — old Doctor Lysander Starr, who was a member of the town council in 1890."

"Good old Doctor Starr!" said our visitor. "His name is still honoured. Well, Mr Holmes, I suppose the only thing we can do is to report to you and let you know how we progress. You will probably hear from us within a day or two." Then the American bowed and went out.

Holmes had lit his pipe, and he sat for some time with a strange smile upon his face.

"Well, what do you think about all that?" I asked at last.

"I am wondering, Watson — just wondering!"

"About what?"

Holmes took his pipe from his lips.

"I was wondering, Watson, what could possibly be the object of this man in telling us such a large number of lies. I nearly asked him what his real purpose was — there are times when a sudden, sharp attack is the best way of dealing with such a person — but I decided that it would be better to let him think he had fooled us. Here is a man with an English coat and English trousers, both showing signs of having been worn for at least a year: and yet according to his pile of papers, and according also to his own account, he is an American from Kansas who has only recently arrived in London. There have been no advertisements about Garridebs. You know that I miss nothing of that sort. The small advertisements have often been useful to me in my cases, and I could not possibly have failed to notice such a one as that. I never knew a Doctor Lysander Starr of Topeka. Almost everything our visitor said was a lie. I think he really is an American, but he has been in London for years, and his voice has gradually become less and less American. What is his object, then? What is the purpose of this extraordinary search for Garridebs? The problem is worth our attention. Clearly this man is a criminal, but he is a strange and imaginative one. We must now find out if our other Garrideb is a liar too. Just ring him up, Watson, please."

I did so, and heard a weak voice, rather like that of a goat, at the other end of the line.

"Yes, yes, I am Mr Nathan Garrideb. Is Mr Holmes there? I should very much like to have a word with Mr Holmes."

My friend took the telephone from me and I heard his half of the conversation that followed.

"Yes, he has been here. I believe you don't know him. . . . How long? . . . Only two days! . . . Yes, yes, of course, to receive five million dollars would be very delightful. Will you be at home this evening? I suppose Mr John Garrideb will not be there? . . . Very good, we will come then. I would rather see you in his absence. . . . Doctor Watson will come with me. . . . Yes, in your letter you mentioned you did not go out often. . . . Well, we shall be with you at about six o'clock. You need not mention it to the American lawyer. . . . Very good. Goodbye!"

On that lovely spring evening, even Little Ryder Street, off the Edgware Road (in the rather dull district near Tyburn, where once men and women had been cruelly put to death in public), looked golden and wonderful in the last sloping rays of the sun. The particular house to which we were directed was a large, old-fashioned eighteenth-century brick building. On the ground floor there were two tall, wide windows: these belonged to the very large living room of our client, who had only the ground floor of the house. As we went up to the door Holmes pointed to the name 'GARRIDEB' on a small brass plate.

"That name plate has been there for years, Watson," he remarked. "Its surface is quite worn, and it has lost its original colour. So at least Garrideb is *his* real name!"

The house had a common hall and staircase, and there were a number of names painted in the hall. Some of these names were those of offices; others were those of private persons. No families lived in the house; the people who lived there were unmarried gentlemen of independent habits. Our client opened the door for us himself and apologised by saying that the woman in charge left at four o'clock. Mr Nathan Garrideb was a very tall, thin man with a bent back. He seemed to be about sixty years old. He had no hair on his head, and the skin of his face looked dull and dead. It was easy to see that he never took any exercise. He wore large round glasses and had a goat's beard: but though he looked rather strange he seemed pleasant.

The room was as odd as Mr Nathan Garrideb himself. It looked like a kind of shop. There were cupboards and glass cases everywhere, crowded with old bones and pieces of stone. On either side of the door there stood a case of flying insects, pinned onto cards. All kinds of things were scattered on a large table in the centre of the room. Among them I noticed several powerful magnifying glasses. As I looked quickly round I was astonished at the number of different subjects Mr Garrideb was interested in. Here was a case of ancient coins. There was a collection of tools from the Stone Age. On a shelf I saw a row of model heads of monkeys or ancient men, with names such as 'Neanderthal', 'Heidelberg', and 'Cromagnon' written on cards below them. It was clear that our client was a collector with many interests. As he stood in front of us now, he held a piece of soft leather in his right hand with which he was polishing a coin.

"From Syracuse. And of the best century," he explained, holding it up. "The quality became much worse later. In my opinion there are no finer coins than Syracusan ones of the right century, though some people prefer those from Alexandria. You will find a chair there, Mr Holmes. One moment, please: I will just put those bones somewhere else. And you, sir — ah, yes, Doctor Watson — would you mind putting that Japanese flower pot out of your way? You see round me all the little interests of my life. My doctor is always telling me I ought to take more exercise, but why should I go out? There are so many things to keep me here! Just to make a proper list of all the things one of these cupboards contains would take at least three months."

Holmes looked round him with interest.

"But do you *never* go out?" he asked.

"Hardly ever. Now and then I take a cab and go and buy some new things for my collections, but otherwise I very seldom leave this room. I am not very strong, and my scientific studies keep me very busy. But you can imagine, Mr Holmes, what a shock — what a *pleasant* shock — it was for me when I heard of this extraordinary piece of good luck. Only òne more Garrideb is needed to make the affair complete, and surely we can find one. I had a brother, but he is dead, and women relatives do not count. But there must surely be other Garridebs in the world. I had heard that you handled strange cases, and that was why I wrote to you. Of course, this American gentleman is quite right, and I should have taken his advice first. But I acted with the best intentions."

"I think you acted very wisely indeed," said Holmes. "But are you really anxious to become the owner of a large piece of land in America?"

"Certainly not, sir. Nothing could tempt me to leave my collection. But this gentleman, Mr John Garrideb, has promised to buy my share of the property from me as soon as we have become the owners of the Garrideb land. Five million dollars was the amount of money he mentioned. There are several things on the market at the present moment which would fill gaps in my collection, but which I cannot buy because I lack a few hundred pounds. Just think what I could do with five million dollars! Why, I already have the beginnings of a great national collection!"

The eyes behind his glasses were shining. It was very clear

that Mr Nathan Garrideb was ready to take any amount of trouble to find the third Garrideb.

"I just called to meet you, Mr Garrideb," said Holmes, "and there is no reason why I should interrupt your studies for more than a few minutes. I like to be in personal touch with my clients. There are very few questions I need ask you, as I have your letter, with its very clear account, in my pocket, and I filled up the gaps when the American gentleman called. I believe that until this week you had no idea of his existence?"

"That is so. He called last Tuesday."

"Did he tell you of his visit to me today?"

"Yes, he came straight here after seeing you. He had been very angry."

"Why should he be angry?"

"He seemed to think that my employing a detective was an insult to him as a man of honour. But he was quite cheerful again when he returned."

"Did he suggest any course of action?"

"No, sir, he did not."

"Has he received, or asked for, any money from you?"

"No, sir, never!"

"And you can see no possible purpose he may have?"

"No, none, except what he has told me — to find a third Garrideb."

"Did you tell him of our appointment this evening?"

"Yes, sir, I did."

Holmes sat in silence for a few moments. I could see that the affair was still a mystery to him.

"Have you any very valuable things in your collection?"

"No, sir. I am not a rich man. It is a good collection, but not a very valuable one."

"You have no fear of thieves?"

"None at all."

"How long have you lived in these rooms?"

"For nearly five years."

Holmes's questions were interrupted by a loud knocking at

the door. As soon as our client opened it the American lawyer burst excitedly into the room.

"Here you are!" he cried, waving a newspaper high in the air. "Mr Nathan Garrideb, I congratulate you! You are a rich man, sir. Our business is happily finished and we have been completely successful. As for you, Mr Holmes, we can only say we are sorry if we have given you any useless trouble."

He handed the newspaper to our client, who stood reading an advertisement which the American had marked. Holmes and I leaned forward and read it over his shoulder. This was it:

HOWARD GARRIDEB, Maker of Agricultural Machinery: steam and hand plows; farmers' carts. Apply to Grosvenor Buildings, Aston, Birmingham.

"Wonderful!" cried our excited host. "So now we have found our third man."

"I had begun making inquiries in Birmingham," said the American, "and my agent there has just sent me this advertisement in a local paper. We must hurry and get in touch with this Mr Howard Garrideb. I have already written to him to say that you will see him in his office tomorrow afternoon at four o'clock."

"You want *me* to see him?" said our host, as if this suggestion were a great shock to him.

"Well, what's *your* opinion, Mr Holmes?" asked Mr John Garrideb. "Don't you think it would be wiser? Here am I, a wandering American with an extraordinary story. Why should Mr Howard Garrideb believe what I tell him? But you, Mr Garrideb, are an Englishman with an honourable position in the world, and he will certainly take what you say seriously. I would go to Birmingham with you if you wished, but I have a very busy day tomorrow — and I could easily come and join you there later if you needed me."

"Why, I have not made such a journey for years!" said Mr Nathan Garrideb.

"It is the easiest little journey in the world, Mr Garrideb. I have already found out the time of your train. You leave at twelve o'clock and should be in Birmingham soon after two. Then you can come back home in the evening. You only have to see this man, explain the matter, and get a signed statement of his existence. Good heavens!" he added a little angrily, "considering that I've come all the way from the centre of America, it's surely a very little thing to ask you to do — to travel a hundred miles in order to find the last of the three Garridebs!"

"Mr John Garrideb is quite right," said Holmes. "I think what he says is very true."

Mr Nathan Garrideb's back seemed to become more bent than ever as he said sadly: "Well, I will go if I must. It is certainly hard for me to refuse you anything, Mr Garrideb, considering the wonderful hope that you have brought into my life."

"Then that is agreed," said Holmes, "and no doubt you will let me have a report as soon as you can."

"I'll see to that," said the American. "Well," he added, looking at his watch, "I must go now. I'll call here tomorrow," he said to Mr Nathan Garrideb, "and see you off at the station. Are you coming my way, Mr Holmes? No? Well, then, goodbye! We may have good news for you tomorrow night."

I noticed that my friend seemed relieved when the American left the room. The thoughtful look had disappeared from his face.

"I wish I could examine your collection, Mr Garrideb," he said. "In my profession all sorts of strange bits of knowledge can often be useful and this room of yours is completely full of unusual knowledge."

Our client seemed to shine with pleasure and his eyes were bright behind his big glasses.

"I had always heard, sir, that you were a very clever, sensible man," he said. "I could show you everything now, if you have the time."

"Unfortunately," Holmes answered, "I have not. But your collections are all so well arranged that they hardly need your personal explanation. If I called here tomorrow, I suppose you would not object to my looking round in your absence?"

"Of course not! You would be very welcome. My rooms will, of course, be shut up, but Mrs Saunders is always in the house until four o'clock and would let you in with her key."

"Well, it so happens that I am free tomorrow afternoon. If you would kindly say a word of explanation to Mrs Saunders I should be very grateful. — Oh, Mr Garrideb, who is the house agent through whom you rented these rooms?"

Our client was astonished at this sudden question.

"Holloway and Steele, in the Edgware Road. But why do you ask?"

"Because I am interested in the history of houses, Mr Garrideb," Holmes replied, laughing. "I was wondering if this one was built in the days of Queen Anne, or of King George the First."

"Oh, King George, without any doubt."

"Really? I should have thought it was built a little earlier. However, I can easily find out for certain. Well, goodbye, Mr Garrideb. I wish you success in your Birmingham journey!"

We saw the house agent's as we walked along the Edgware Road, but it was closed for the day, so we made our way back to Baker Street. It was not until after dinner that Holmes mentioned the Garrideb affair again.

"Our little problem is nearly solved," he said. "No doubt you too have worked it out in your own mind."

"I don't understand it at all, Holmes," I replied.

"Everything will be clear tomorrow. Did you notice nothing strange about that advertisement?"

"I saw that the word 'plough' was wrongly spelt."

"Oh, you did notice that, did you? I congratulate you, Watson: you improve all the time. Yes, 'plow' is bad English but good American. The printer had copied the advertisement exactly as he received it. It was in fact an American advertisement, but we were expected to believe that it was put in by an Englishman. How do you explain that?"

"I can only suppose that this American lawyer put the advertisement in himself. But I have no idea what his object in doing so can have been."

"Well, there are three possible explanations. One thing is very clear: he wanted good old Mr Nathan Garrideb to go off to Birmingham. Of course I could have told the old man that his journey was useless. But I decided it would be better to let him go, and allow the affair to develop according to the intentions of the Kansas lawyer. Tomorrow, Watson — tomorrow will be a day of action!"

Holmes was up and out early the next morning. When he returned at lunch time I noticed a very serious expression on his face.

"This is a more dangerous affair than I had expected, Watson," he said. "I had to warn you, though I know that the danger will only be an extra attraction to you! I think I know my Watson by now. But there *is* danger, and you should realise this."

"Well, this will not be the first danger that we have shared, Holmes. And I hope it will not be the last! What is the particular danger this time?"

"I have found out who Mr John Garrideb , the Kansas lawyer, really is. He is the murderer 'Killer' Evans — an evil and terrible man."

"I am afraid I have never heard of him."

"Ah, it is not part of your profession to carry about a kind of 'Encyclopedia of Crime' in your memory! I have been down to see our friend Lestrade at Scotland Yard. The London police may lack imagination, but they are remarkably thorough, and I had an idea that I might get on the track of our 'Mr John Garrideb' by looking through their records. I soon found a photograph of his round, smiling face. The names underneath were James Winter, Morecroft, and 'Killer' Evans." Holmes pulled out an envelope from his pocket. "I noted down a few of the other points about him. He is forty-four years old. He was born in Chicago. He is known to have shot three men in the United States. But he got out of prison by means of political influence. He came to London in 1893. In January 1895 he shot a man in a quarrel over a card game in a night club in the Waterloo Road. The man died, but it was proved that he had started the fight. The dead man was Rodger Prescott, who was famous as a forger in Chicago. 'Killer' Evans was sent to prison, but came out last year. Since then the police have been watching his movements, but he seems to have been leading an honest life. He is a very dangerous man, usually carries a gun, and is not afraid to shoot. That is our man, Watson!"

"But what is his object in this Garrideb affair?" I asked.

"Well, that is becoming clearer. I have been to the house agent's. Mr Nathan Garrideb, as he told us, has been at Little Ryder Street for five years. The rooms were empty for a year before then. Before that, they were let to a mysterious gentleman called Waldron. Waldron's appearance was well remembered at the office. He had suddenly disappeared and nothing more had been heard of him. He was a tall, very dark man with a beard. Now, Prescott, the man whom 'Killer' Evans shot, was, according to our friends at Scotland Yard, also a tall, dark man with a beard. My guess is that Prescott, the American criminal, used to live in Little Ryder Street, in the room where old Mr Garrideb keeps his collection. So at last we have a connection, you see."

"And where is the next clue?"

"Well, we must go now and look for that."

He took a gun from the drawer and handed it to me.

"I have my own gun with me," he said. "If 'Killer' Evans begins shooting we must be prepared. I'll give you an hour for your afternoon sleep, Watson, and then I think it will be time for our Little Ryder Street adventure."

It was just four o'clock when we reached Mr Nathan Garrideb's strange home. Mrs Saunders was about to leave, but she had no hesitation about admitting us, as the door shut with a spring lock and Holmes promised to make sure that everything was safe before we left. Soon afterwards the front door of the house closed and we saw Mrs Saunders pass the windows. We were now alone in the lower part of the house. Holmes made a rapid examination of the rooms. There was one cupboard in a dark corner which stood out a little from the wall. It was behind this that we hid, while Holmes spoke to me in a whisper.

"Evans wanted to get the old gentleman out of his room — that is very clear; but as the collector never went out, the 'Killer's' problem was not an easy one. It seems that all his lies about the Garrideb will and the Garrideb land had no other purpose than to get Mr Nathan Garrideb away from the house for one day. One has to admit, Watson, that the 'Killer's' lies did have a certain cleverness about them — though the old collector's unusual name gave him an opportunity which he could hardly have expected."

"But what can the 'Killer' possibly want here?" I asked.

"Well, that is what we are here to find out. I don't think it has anything whatever to do with our client. It is something connected with the man that Evans killed — a man who may have joined with him in criminal activities of some kind. There is some guilty secret in this room, I think. At first I thought Mr Nathan Garrideb might have something in his collection that was more valuable than he realised — something worth the attention of a big criminal. But when I discovered that the wicked Rodger Prescott used to live here I realised that there must be some quite different explanation. Well, Watson, the only thing we can do now is to have patience and wait and watch."

A few moments later we heard the front door of the house open and shut. Then there was the sound of a key in the lock, and the American was in the room. He closed the door quietly behind him, gave a sharp look round the room to see that everything was safe, threw off his coat, and walked up to the table in the centre of the room with the firm step of a man who knows exactly what he has to do and how to do it. He pushed the table to one side and pulled up the square of carpet on which it stood. Then he rolled the carpet completely back, took a thief's tool from his inside pocket, and knelt down to work on the floor. A moment later we heard the sound of sliding boards, and a square hole appeared in the floor. 'Killer' Evans struck a match, lit a lamp, and disappeared down the hole.

This was clearly our opportunity. Holmes touched my wrist as a signal, and together we moved quietly across the room to the hole in the boards. In spite of our efforts to make no noise, however, Evans must have heard a slight sound as we passed over the old floorboards, for his head suddenly came up out of the open space and he looked anxiously round. When he saw us a look of anger, disappointment, and hatred appeared on his face. This gradually changed to his old broad smile as he realised that two guns were aimed at his head.

"Well, well!" he said, coolly, as he climbed up out of the hole. "You have been too clever for me, Mr Holmes. I suppose you realised from the first that I was telling lies. Well, sir, I congratulate you: you have beaten me and ———"

In an instant he had pulled out a gun from an inside pocket and had fired two shots. I felt a sudden hot tearing pain, as if a red-hot iron had been pressed against the top of my leg. There was a crash as Holmes's gun came down on Evans's head. I saw the man lying on the floor with blood running down his face, while Holmes searched him for weapons. Then my friend's thin but strong arms were round me and he was leading me to a chair.

"You're not hurt, Watson? Oh, please say that you're not hurt!"

I did not mind the the wound — I would not have minded many wounds — for if I had not been hit I should never have known the extraordinary loyalty and love that Holmes felt for me — feelings which he always hid under his cold outward manner. For a moment I saw tears in those clear, hard eyes of his; and the firm lips were shaking. I suddenly realised that Holmes had a great heart as well as a great mind. That moment of realisation was my reward for years of humble service.

"It's nothing, Holmes. It's just a small wound."

He had made a long tear in my trousers with his pocket knife.

"You are right!" he cried — and I could hear the relief in his voice. "The skin is scarcely broken." He turned to our prisoner and gave him a cold, scornful look. "It is a lucky thing for you. If you had killed Watson, you would not have got out of this room alive. Now, sir, what have you got to say?"

He had nothing to say. He only lay there and looked at us with a child's anger. I leaned on Holmes's arm, and together we looked down into the small cellar at the bottom of the hole in the floor. It was still lit by the lamp which Evans had taken down with him. We saw a mass of rusty machinery, great rolls of paper, a quantity of bottles, and — tidily arranged upon a small table — a number of neat little piles.

"A printing press — for printing forged paper money," said Holmes.

"Yes, sir," said our prisoner, struggling to his feet and then sinking into a chair. "Prescott was the greatest forger there has ever been in London, and that's his machine, and those bundles on the table are two thousand of his bank notes. Each of them is worth a hundred pounds and is good enough to fool anybody. Help yourselves, gentlemen, and let me go. Let's make a deal!"

Holmes laughed.

"We don't do things like that in this country, Mr Evans. You shot this man Prescott, didn't you?"

"Yes, sir, and I was sent to prison for five years for doing it, though it was he who drew his gun first. Five years in prison! — when I ought to have been given a ribbon and a reward by the King! There isn't a man living who could see the difference between a Prescott note and a Bank of England one, and if I hadn't killed him he would have filled London with them. I was the only man in the world who knew where he made them. Can you blame me for wanting to get to the place? And when I found the old bone-collector with the odd name sitting right on top of it, of course I had to do what I could to get rid of him. Perhaps it would have been wiser simply to shoot him. It would have been very easy to do that, but I have a soft heart and can't begin shooting unless the other man has a gun too. But, Mr Holmes, what have I done wrong, anyhow? I haven't used that machinery down there. I haven't hurt old Mr Garrideb. What crime are you arresting me for?"

"Only attempted murder, I think," said Holmes. "But that isn't our job. It will be a matter for Scotland Yard. Just ring them up, Watson, would you, please? The call won't be entirely unexpected."

So those were the facts about 'Killer' Evans and his remarkable invention of the three Garridebs. We heard later that poor old Mr Nathan Garrideb never got over the shock of his disappointment. He went mad and was taken away to a special hospital in Brixton.

It was a happy day at Scotland Yard when the Prescott machinery was discovered, for, though they knew that it existed, they had never been able, after Prescott's death, to find out where it was. Many high officials at the Yard could now sleep more peacefully at night, and felt so grateful to Evans for leading them to Prescott's cellar that they would willingly have given him the reward of which he had spoken. However, at Evans's trial the judge took a less favourable view of the case, and the 'Killer' was sent back to the prison which he had so recently left.

# The Adventure of Wisteria Lodge

It was a cold and windy day towards the end of March. Sherlock
Holmes and I were sitting at lunch when there was a knock at
the door and our landlady brought in a telegram. Holmes read
it and quickly wrote a reply, but said nothing to me about it.
The matter must have remained in his thoughts, however, as he
kept looking at the telegram. At last, after lunch, he read it
aloud to me:

"HAVE JUST HAD AN EXTRAORDINARY EXPERIENCE.
MAY I COME AND SEE YOU? — SCOTT ECCLES, POST
OFFICE, CHARING CROSS."

"Is Scott Eccles a man or a woman?" I asked.

"Oh, a man, of course! No woman would ever send a telegram
like that. A woman would have come straight to me."

"And did you agree to see Mr Scott Eccles?"

"My dear Watson, need you ask? Brain work is always
absolutely necessary to me." Just then there was the sound of
footsteps on the stairs. "Ah! here comes our client now."

Our visitor was tall, fat and very solemn. His grey hair was
sticking out and his red face seemed to be swollen with anger.

"I have had a very strange and unpleasant experience, Mr
Holmes," he said at once, "And I have come to you for an
explanation!"

"Please sit down, Mr Scott Eccles," said Holmes gently. "Now
tell me exactly why you have come to me."

"Well, sir, there has been no crime, and so I could not go to the
police. Of course I have never had any dealings with a private
detective before, but ———"

"And secondly," Holmes interrupted, "why didn't you come at
once?"

"What do you mean?" asked Mr Scott Eccles.

Holmes looked at his watch. "It is now a quarter past two," he said. "Your telegram was sent from Charing Cross at about one o'clock. And yet your clothing and appearance show that your disturbing experience happened as soon as you woke up this morning."

Our client looked down at his untidy clothes and felt his rough chin.

"You are right, Mr Holmes. I had no time to think about my appearance this morning. I wanted to get out of that house as quickly as I could! But I made some inquiries of my own before coming to you. I went to the house agents' first. They told me that Mr Garcia had paid his rent and that everything was in order at Wisteria Lodge."

"My dear sir," Holmes said with a laugh, "you are like my friend Doctor Watson, who has a bad habit of beginning his stories at the end. Please arrange your thoughts and then begin at the beginning."

There was an interruption, however. Mrs Hudson showed Tobias Gregson and another police officer into the room. Gregson was a Scotland Yard detective. He shook hands with Holmes, and introduced the other officer as Mr Baynes of the Surrey police. Then he turned to Mr Scott Eccles.

"Are you Mr John Scott Eccles, of Popham House, Lee?"

"Yes, I am."

"We have been following you about all the morning."

"But why? What do you want?" asked our client.

"We want a statement from you," said Gregson, "about the death of Mr Aloysius Garcia, of Wisteria Lodge, near Esher."

Mr Scott Eccles's face was white now. "Dead? Did you say he was dead?"

"Yes, sir, he died last night."

"But how did he die? Was it an accident?"

"It was murder, without any doubt."

"Oh God! This is terrible! But surely you can't suspect *me*!"

"A letter of yours was found in the dead man's pocket. It shows that you were intending to spend last night at his house."

"And so I did."

"Ah!" Gregson took out his notebook.

"Wait a moment, Gregson," said Holmes. "You want a plain statement from Mr Scott Eccles, don't you? He was going to give us one when you arrived. Give our client a glass of brandy, please, Watson. Now, sir, please try to forget the presence of these police officers and tell us everything."

Our visitor swallowed his brandy and the colour began to return to his face.

"I am unmarried," he began, "and I have many friends. One of these is Mr Melville, a retired gentleman who lives in Kensington. A few weeks ago I went to dinner at the Melvilles' and they introduced me to a young man called Garcia. He told me that he belonged to the Spanish Government office in London. He spoke perfect English, however. He was very good-looking and had excellent manners. He seemed to like me very much, and only two days later he came to see me at Lee. Before long he invited me to spend a few days at his house, Wisteria Lodge, between Esher and Oxshott in Surrey. I arranged to begin my visit yesterday evening.

"Garcia had already described his household to me. There was a faithful Spanish servant and an excellent American-Indian cook.

"I hired a cab at Esher Station. Wisteria Lodge is about two miles away, on the south side of the village. It is quite a big house, in its own grounds, but is in extremely poor condition.

"Garcia opened the door to me himself, and gave me a very friendly welcome. Then the Spanish servant showed me to my bedroom. He seemed as dark and sad as the house itself.

"At dinner I was the only guest. Garcia did his best to entertain me, but I could see that his thoughts were wandering. He bit his nails and kept drumming with his fingers on the table. He seemed to be full of impatience. The meal itself was neither well cooked nor well served. Many times that evening I wished I was back at home.

"Towards the end of dinner the servant brought Garcia a note. I noticed that my host seemed even more inattentive and strange after he had read it. He no longer attempted to make conversation, but only sat and smoked. At about eleven o'clock I went with relief to bed. Some time later Garcia looked in at my door and asked me if I had rung the bell. I said that I had not. He apologised for having disturbed me so late: he told me it was nearly one o'clock. When he had gone I fell asleep and did not wake up until almost nine. I had asked the Spanish servant to call me at eight, and I was surprised at his forgetfulness. I jumped out of bed and rang the bell. Nobody came. I rang again and again, but still nothing happened. I thought that perhaps the bell was out of order. I dressed quickly and then ran angrily downstairs to order some hot water, but there was no one there. I shouted in the hall. There was no answer. Then I ran from room to room. There was nobody anywhere. I knocked at Garcia's bedroom door. No reply. I turned the handle and walked in. The room was empty, and the bed had not been slept in. He too had gone! The foreign host, the foreign servant, the foreign cook — all had disappeared in the night! That was the end of my visit to Wisteria Lodge."

Sherlock Holmes rubbed his hands with delight. "And what did you do next?" he asked.

"I was very angry. At first I thought it was a practical joke. I packed my bag, left the house, and walked into Esher. I called at Allan Brothers', the main house agents in the village, and asked some questions about Mr Garcia and Wisteria Lodge. I thought that perhaps Garcia had gone away suddenly in order to avoid paying the rent. But the agents thanked me for warning them, and told me that Garcia had paid several months' rent in advance. Then I returned to London and made some inquiries at the Spanish Government office. The man was unknown there. After this I went to see Melville, at whose house I had first met Garcia, but he really knew very little about the man. Then I sent that telegram to you. A friend of mine had mentioned your name to me: he said you gave advice in difficult cases." Mr Scott Eccles turned now to Gregson. "I have told the whole truth, officer. I know absolutely nothing more about Mr Garcia and his death. I only want to help the police in every possible way."

"I'm sure of it, Mr Scott Eccles," answered Gregson. "Your story agrees perfectly with all the facts of the case. For example, there was that note which arrived during dinner at Wisteria Lodge. What did Garcia do with it after he had read it?"

"He rolled it up and threw it into the fire."

"Well, Mr Baynes?" asked Gregson, turning to the other police officer. Baynes was a country detective, a fat man with a red face and bright, clever eyes. He smiled and took a small piece of paper out of his pocket. It was brown in places.

"Garcia threw badly," he said. "The letter was only slightly burnt, as it fell into the fireplace and not into the fire. Shall I read it aloud to these gentlemen, Mr Gregson?"

"Certainly, Mr Baynes."

"It says: 'Our own colours, green and white. Green open, white shut. Main stairs, first passage, seventh on the right, green door. — D.' It is addressed on the other side to Mr Garcia, Wisteria Lodge. The letter is in a woman's handwriting, but we think the address was written by someone else."

"But what has happened to Garcia?" asked Mr Scott Eccles impatiently.

"He was found dead this morning in a field near Oxshott, about a mile from his home. All the bones in his head had been crushed by several blows from some large heavy weapon. It's a lonely place, and the nearest house is a quarter of a mile away."

"Had he been robbed?" asked Holmes.

"No, there was no attempt at robbery," replied Baynes.

"All this is very painful and terrible," said Mr Scott Eccles, "but why am *I* mixed up in the affair?"

"Because the only paper in Mr Garcia's pocket was your letter, sir," answered Baynes. "It was the envelope of this letter which gave us the dead man's name and address. When we reached his house at half past nine this morning we found neither you nor anyone else inside. Mr Gregson tracked you down at Charing Cross Post Office by means of your telegram."

"And now, sir," said Gregson, "you must come with us to Scotland Yard and give us your statement in writing."

"Certainly, I will come at once. But I am still your client, Mr Holmes. I want to know the truth about this affair!"

"Mr Baynes, do you know exactly when the man was killed?" asked Holmes.

"He had been lying in the field since one o'clock. There was rain at about that time, and the murder certainly happened before the rain."

"But that is quite impossible, Mr Baynes!" cried our client. "He spoke to me in my bedroom at one o'clock."

"It is certainly strange," said Sherlock Holmes with a smile, "but not impossible."

"Have you formed any opinion about this affair, Watson?" asked Holmes, later the same afternoon.

"As the servants have disappeared, I think that perhaps they were concerned in the crime," I said.

"It is possible," he said. "But why should they attack him on the one night when he had a guest?"

"But why did they run away?" I objected.

"That, Watson, is the problem. Mr Scott Eccles's strange experience is also a mystery. Why should a charming young man like Garcia want the friendship of a rather stupid middle-aged person like Scott Eccles? What is Scott Eccles's most noticeable quality? He is clearly an honest man, an old-fashioned Englishman whom other Englishmen believe and trust. You saw how those two policemen accepted his extraordinary story! Garcia wanted him as a witness, Watson."

"But what was he to witness?"

"He could have sworn that his host was at home at one o'clock this morning. When Garcia told him it was one it was probably no later than midnight."

"What is your explanation of the message? 'Our own colours, green and white . . . ' "

"That sounds like a horse-race," Holmes replied. "And 'green open, white shut' must be a signal. The rest of the note seems to be an appointment. There may be a jealous husband somewhere in this case. Then there is the signature — 'D'."

"The man was a Spaniard. I suggest that 'D' stands for Dolores, a common female name in Spain."

"Good, Watson, very good — but quite impossible. A Spaniard would write to another Spaniard in Spanish. The writer of this note is certainly English. The affair is still very mysterious. Meanwhile I have sent a telegram which may bring us some helpful information."

When the answer to Holmes's telegram came he passed it across to me. It was only a list of names and addresses. "'Lord Harringby,'" I read, "'The Dingle; Sir George Ffolliott, Oxshott Towers; Mr Hynes, Purdey Place; Mr James Baker-Williams, Forton Old Hall; Mr Henderson, High Gable; Mr Joshua Stone, Nether Walsling.' I don't quite understand, Holmes."

"My dear fellow, have you forgotten the message that 'D' sent to Garcia? 'Main stairs, first passage, seventh on the right . . . ' The house we are looking for has more than one staircase, and one of the passages contains at least seven doors. It must be a very large house, Watson, and it is probably within a mile or two of Oxshott. My telegram was to Allan Brothers', the house agents. I asked them to send me a list of all the large houses in the Oxshott district, and here it is."

We went down by train to Esher later in the afternoon and took rooms at the village inn. We went along to Wisteria Lodge with Mr Baynes that evening. The house was in darkness except for a weak light in one window on the ground floor.

"There's a policeman inside," Baynes explained. "I'll knock at the window." He crossed the lawn and knocked on the glass. I heard a cry of alarm and saw a policeman jump up nervously from his chair. A moment later he opened the front door to us. The candle in his hand was trembling violently.

"What's the matter, Walters?" asked Baynes.

"I am glad you have come, sir. It has been a long wait, and it's a lonely, silent house. I don't like those horrible things in the kitchen either. And when you tapped at the window I thought the devil had come again."

"What do you mean?" Baynes asked sharply.

"The devil, sir. It was at the window."

"What was at the window, and when?"

"It was about two hours ago. It was just beginning to get dark. I was reading. I don't know what made me look up, but there was a horrible face at the window. I shall see it in my dreams, sir. I know I shall."

"A policeman should never talk in that silly way, Walters."

"I know, sir. But it really frightened me. It wasn't black, sir, and it wasn't white. It was a kind of pale brownish grey — a whitish mud colour. And it was enormous, sir — twice the size of your face. And it had huge eyes, and great white teeth like a wild animal's."

"I think you must have been dreaming, Walters!" said Baynes.

"We can easily find out," said Holmes. He lit his small pocket lamp and looked closely at the surface of the lawn outside the window. "Yes, a size 12 shoe, I think. He must have been an enormous fellow."

"Where did he go?" I asked.

"He seems to have forced his way through this hedge."

"Well," said Baynes, "we have other things to think of now, Mr Holmes. Let me show you the kitchen."

This was a high, dark room at the back of the house. We saw a pile of straw and few bedclothes. It appeared that the cook slept there. The table was covered with dirty plates and half-eaten food — the remains of the meal which Mr Scott Eccles had shared the previous evening.

"Look at this," said Baynes. "What do you think it is?"

He held up his candle to let us see an extraordinary object on top of a cupboard. It was a black, leathery, dried-up thing shaped like a baby or a monkey. A double band of sea shells was fastened round it.

"Very interesting!" said Holmes. "Very interesting indeed! Is there anything else?"

In silence Baynes led the way to the other side of the kitchen and held out his candle. There, on a small table, we saw the legs, wings, head and body of a large white bird. The feathers were still on, but the bird had been torn to pieces.

"Extremely odd!" said Holmes. "It is really a very unusual case."

Mr Baynes had kept the most horrible thing of all until the last. He bent down and pulled a bucket out from under the small table. It was full of blood.

"We also found some burnt bones," he said. "A young goat seems to have been killed here. A young goat and a white bird."

"Very odd indeed," said Holmes. "Very odd and interesting. Well, there is nothing more for me to do here. Thank you, Mr Baynes. Good night and good luck!"

Holmes told me nothing of the results of his inquiries in the next few days. One day he visited the London Library, but he spent most of his time in country walks around Esher and Oxshott. He pretended to be a scientist collecting rare plants, but he spent many hours in conversation with the village people. His plant box was usually almost empty in the evenings when he came back to the Bull Inn.

About five days after the crime I opened my morning paper and saw in large letters:

THE OXSHOTT MYSTERY.
A SOLUTION.
MURDERER ARRESTED.

When I read this out to Holmes he jumped out of his chair as if he had been stung.

"Good heavens!" he cried. "So Baynes has got him?"

"It appears that he has," I replied, and read the report aloud to him. "'Great excitement was caused in Esher and the neighbouring district last night when a man was arrested in connection with the Oxshott murder. Our readers will remember that Mr Garcia, of Wisteria Lodge, was found dead near Oxshott last week. His body showed signs of extreme violence. On the same night his servant and his cook disappeared. Their flight seemed to show that they had something to do with the murder. The police thought that the dead man might have had gold or jewels in the house, and that robbery was the real reason for the crime. Mr Baynes of the Surrey police made great efforts to track the two servants down. He believed that they had not gone far, and that it would be easy to find their hiding place. The cook in particular was a man of very noticeable appearance, a huge yellowish foreigner with an enormous and very ugly face. This man was seen by Policeman Walters at Wisteria Lodge on the day after the crime. After this Mr Baynes decided to remove his men from the house to the grounds, where they hid behind the trees every evening. The cook walked into this trap last night. In the struggle Policeman Downing was badly bitten, but the man was arrested and taken to the police station. We are told that the prisoner has been charged with the murder of Mr Garcia.'"

"We must see Baynes at once!" cried Holmes, picking up his hat.

The house where Baynes was staying was only a short distance away. We hurried down the village street and found that he was just leaving his lodgings.

"You've seen the paper, Mr Holmes?" he asked, holding one out to us.

"Yes, Baynes, I've seen it. Please don't be angry with me if I give you a word of friendly warning."

"Of warning, Mr Holmes?"

"I have looked into the case very carefully, and I think you may be making a mistake. I don't want you to do anything unless you are sure."

"You're very kind, Mr Holmes."

"I am only speaking for your own good."

It seemed to me that Mr Baynes closed one of his tiny eyes for a moment and gave a slight smile.

"You have your methods, Mr Holmes, and I have mine."

"Oh, very good," said Holmes. "But don't blame me if things go wrong."

"No, sir. I believe you mean well. But I am dealing with this case in my own way."

"Let us say no more about it."

"Meanwhile let me tell you about the cook. He's a wild man, as strong as a cart-horse and as fierce as the devil. He nearly bit Downing's thumb off before they could master him. He hardly speaks a word of English, and only makes noises in his throat like an animal."

"And you think that he murdered his master?"

"I didn't say so, Mr Holmes; I didn't say so. We all have our little methods. You can try yours and I will try mine."

"I don't understand Baynes at all," said Holmes as we walked away together. "He seems to have gone completely wrong. Well, as he says, each of us must try his own way. We shall see the results!"

When we were back in our sitting room at the Bull Inn, Holmes pushed me into an armchair.

"I have many things to tell you about this case, Watson," he said. "And I may need your help tonight."

"First of all," he went on, "I have been thinking about the letter Garcia received on the evening of the murder. We can dismiss the idea that his servants had anything to do with his death. It was Garcia who was planning a crime that night. It was he who invited Scott Eccles, that perfect witness. And it was he who lied to him about the time. I believe Garcia died in the course of a criminal adventure."

"Who, then," Holmes continued, "is most likely to have taken his life? Surely the person against whom Garcia's criminal plan was directed.

"We can now see a reason for the disappearance of Garcia's household. They were *all* concerned in his plan. If the plan had succeeded Garcia would have returned home and Scott Eccles would have been useful to him as a witness. All would have been well. But the attempt was a dangerous one, and if Garcia did *not* return by a certain time the servants would know he was probably dead. It had been arranged, therefore, that in such a case they would escape to their hiding place. In that hiding place they could make another attempt to carry the plan into effect. That would fully explain the facts, wouldn't it?"

The mystery seemed much clearer to me now. I wondered, as I always did with Holmes, why I had not thought of the explanation myself.

"But why should one of the servants return to Wisteria Lodge?" I objected.

"I think that perhaps in the confusion of flight something precious, something he could not bear to lose, had been left behind. That would explain both his visits, wouldn't it?"

"Yes, you're right," I said. "But you were going to tell me about the note that Garcia received at dinner on the evening of the murder."

"Ah, yes. That note shows that the woman who wrote it was concerned in the plan too. But where was she? I have already shown you that the place could only be some large house, and that the number of large houses is limited. Since we arrived in Esher I have looked at all these houses and made inquiries about their owners. One house, and only one, especially attracted my attention. This was the famous old house called High Gable, one mile out of Oxshott on the farther side. High Gable is less than half a mile from the place where Garcia's body was found. The other big houses belong to ordinary, old-fashioned people to whom nothing exciting ever happens. But Mr Henderson, of High Gable, is certainly an unusual man

— a man who would be likely to have strange adventures. I therefore decided to give all my attention to Mr Henderson and his household.

"They are a strange set of people, Watson. The man himself is the strangest of them all. I managed to think of a reason for asking to see him. But I think he guessed my real purpose. He is about fifty years old, strong and active, with grey hair, thick black eyebrows, and dark, deep-set, troubled eyes. He is a tough, fierce, masterful man with the spirit of a king. Either he is a foreigner or else he has spent most of his life in very hot countries. His face is like yellow leather. There is no doubt that his friend and secretary, Mr Lucas, is a foreigner. *His* face is the colour of milk chocolate. He is a cat-like person with a very gentle, polite voice. But he is completely evil, I am sure. You see, Watson, we now know of two separate sets of foreigners — one at Wisteria Lodge and the other at High Gable. I think we shall find the solution of our mystery in the connection between these two groups.

"Henderson and Lucas, who are close and trusted friends, are at the centre of the High Gable household. But there is one other person who may be even more important to us in our present inquiries. Henderson has two young daughters. One is thirteen and the other is eleven. They are taught by a lady called Miss Burnet. She is an Englishwoman, about forty years old. I am particularly interested in Miss Burnet, Watson. There is also one personal servant — a man.

"This little group forms the real family. They all travel about together. Henderson is a great traveller. He is always on the move. It is only within the last few weeks that he has returned to High Gable after being away for a whole year. He is extremely rich, you see. He can easily afford to satisfy any desire as soon as he becomes conscious of it.

"The house is full of other servants of every kind. You know what the servants of a large English country house are like. They have very little work to do but they eat meat four times a day!

"Servants can be very useful to a detective, however. There is no better way of getting information than making friends with one of them. I was lucky enough to find a former gardener of Henderson's. His name is John Warner. Henderson dismissed him recently in a moment of temper. Luckily Warner still has friends among the High Gable servants, who all greatly fear and dislike their master. So I had a key to all the secrets of the household.

"And what a strange household it is, Watson! I don't understand everything yet, but it is certainly odd. The house is in two wings. The servants live on one side and the family on the other. The only connection between the two is Henderson's own personal servant, who serves the family's meals. Everything is carried to a certain door in the servants' wing. This door is the only one that communicates with the other wing of the house. The girls and their teacher hardly ever go out, except into the garden. And Henderson never goes out alone. His dark secretary is like his shadow. The servants say that their master is terribly afraid of something. Warner says that he has sold his soul to the devil in exchange for money. 'The master's afraid that the ground will open and that the devil will come up out of hell to claim him!' he says. Nobody knows where the Hendersons came from, or who they are. They are very violent people. Twice Henderson has struck people with his whip, and has had to pay them a lot of money in order to keep out of the courts.

"Well, now, Watson, all this new information should help us to judge the situation. It seems certain that the letter came out of this strange household. I believe it was an invitation to Garcia to carry out some attempt which had already been planned. Who can have written the note? It was someone inside the house, and it was a woman. Isn't the only possible person Miss Burnet, the teacher? All our reasoning seems to support that idea. Miss Burnet's age and character, however, make any idea of a love affair impossible.

"If she wrote the note she must have been concerned in her

friend Garcia's plot. Now he died in trying to carry out that plot. So she must have felt great bitterness and hatred against their enemies. She must want revenge, Watson. Could we see her, then, and try to use her?

"That was my first thought. But Miss Burnet has not been seen since the night of the murder. She has completely disappeared. Is she still alive? Or was she perhaps killed on the night of Garcia's death? Or is she only being kept prisoner somewhere? If so, her life may still be in danger.

"Unfortunately the police cannot help us here. It would not be possible to get a search warrant. We still lack proof. So I am watching the house. I am employing Warner to stand on guard at the gates.

"We can't let this situation continue, however. If the law can do nothing we must take the risk ourselves."

"What do you suggest?" I asked.

"I know which is Miss Burnet's room. There is a low roof outside the window. My suggestion is that you and I go there tonight and climb in."

This idea did not seem very attractive to me. The thought of that old house with its alarming owner and its connections with violent death made me hesitate. And I did not really want to break the law. But I could never refuse Holmes anything. His reasoning always persuaded me. This time I knew that his plan was the only way of solving the mystery of Garcia's death. I pressed his hand in silence to show that I would be ready for the wildest adventure.

But our inquiries did not have such an adventurous ending. It was about five o'clock, and the shadows of the March evening were beginning to come down, when an excited countryman rushed into our sitting room.

"They've gone, Mr Holmes. They went by the last train. The lady broke away, and I've got her in a cab down below."

"Excellent, Warner!" cried Holmes, springing to his feet. "We shall know the solution very soon now, Watson."

The woman in the cab seemed to be very weak and tired. Her

head hung down on her breast, but she slowly raised it to look up at us. Her face was thin and sad. In the centre of each of her dull eyes I saw the signs of opium. She had been drugged!

"I watched the gate, as you told me to, Mr Holmes," said Warner. "When the carriage came out I followed it to the station. She was like a person walking in her sleep. But when they tried to get her into the train she came to life and struggled. They pushed her in, but she fought her way out again. I took her arm and helped her. I got her into a cab, and here we are. I shan't easily forget the master's face at the window of that train! I could see murder in his eyes. The black-eyed, yellow devil!"

We carried Miss Burnet upstairs and laid her on one of the beds. Two cups of the strongest coffee quickly cleared her brain of opium.

Mr Baynes, whom we had sent for at once, shook Holmes by the hand. "Well done, Mr Holmes! I was on the same scent as you from the first."

"What! You were after Henderson?"

"That's right. While you were hiding in the garden at High Gable I was up in one of the trees. I saw you down below."

"Then why did you arrest Garcia's cook?"

Baynes laughed.

"I arrested the wrong man in order to make Henderson think he was safe," he said. "He would think we weren't watching him. I knew he would be likely to run away then. That would give us a chance of getting hold of Miss Burnet."

"Tell me, Baynes, who *is* Henderson?"

"Henderson is really Juan Murillo, who was once known as the Animal of San Pedro. He was an evil Central American ruler who escaped from the State of San Pedro after the revolution, taking with him many of the national treasures. He was a cruel, fearless robber and everybody hated him.

"Yes," Baynes continued, "he escaped. He completely disappeared, and none of his enemies knew where he was. But they wanted revenge, and they never rested until they found him.

"The national colours of San Pedro are green and white, as in Miss Burnet's letter. Murillo called himself Henderson, but he had other names in Paris and Rome and Madrid and Barcelona, where his ship arrived from South America in 1886. His enemies have only recently found his hiding place."

"They discovered him a year ago," said Miss Burnet, who had sat up and was listening with keen attention. "This time the noble Garcia has been killed, but before long our plot will succeed and the Animal of San Pedro will be put to death!" Her thin hands tightened with the violence of her hatred.

"But why are you mixed up in these foreign political affairs, Miss Burnet?" Holmes asked. "One does not expect to find an English lady concerned in murder and plots."

"I *must* take part!" she cried. "Through me this criminal will be punished. Justice will be done. He has done many murders and stolen many treasures. To you his robberies and murders are like crimes that are done on some other planet. But *we* know. We have learned the truth in sorrow and in suffering. To us there is no devil in hell as bad as Juan Murillo. For us there can be no peace until we have had our revenge."

"No doubt he was a very wicked ruler," said Holmes. "But how are you concerned in the affairs of the State of San Pedro?"

"I will tell you everything. My real name is Mrs Victor Durando. My husband was the London representative of the San Pedro Government. He met me and married me in this country. Oh, he was a noble being! And because he was so noble Murillo had him shot. All his property was taken away too.

"Then came the revolution. A secret society was formed with the purpose of punishing Juan Murillo for all his crimes. At last we managed to find out that Mr Henderson of High Gable, Oxshott, was really the Animal of San Pedro. I was given the job of joining his household and watching all his movements. I smiled at him, did my duty to his children, and waited. The society had attempted to kill him in Paris once before, but the attempt failed.

"It was not easy to plan our revenge. Aloysius Garcia and

his two servants, all of whom had suffered under the evil rule of Murillo, came to live in the district. But Garcia could do little during the day, as the Animal was very careful. He never went out alone. His friend Lucas, whose real name is Lopez, always went with him. At night, however, he slept alone. This gave us our chance. We arranged to make our attempt on a certain evening. Murillo often changed his bedroom, and it was necessary to send Garcia a note on the day itself. The signal of a green light in a window would mean that the doors were open and that it was safe. A white light would mean 'Don't come in tonight'.

"But everything went wrong for us. Lopez, the secretary, became suspicious. He crept up behind me as I was writing the note, and sprang upon me as soon as I had finished it. He and his master dragged me to my room, and then discussed whether or not to murder me with their knives there and then. In the end they decided that it would be too dangerous. But Garcia must die! Murillo twisted my arm until I gave them the address. Lopez addressed the note which I had written. Then he sent José, the confidential servant, with it. Murillo must have  done the murder, as Lopez remained to guard me.

"After that terrible night, they kept me locked in my room. Oh! they treated me very cruelly. Look at these red marks on my arms! Once I tried to call out from the window, but they covered my mouth with a thick cloth. For five days this cruel treatment continued. They hardly gave me any food. This afternoon a good meal was brought in to me, but it must have contained opium. The journey to the station was like a dream. But my energy came back at the station and I managed to break away, with the help of that kind gardener."

About six months later Lord Montalva and Mr Rulli, his secretary, were murdered in their rooms at the Hotel Escurial in Madrid. The murderers were never arrested. Mr Baynes came to see us in Baker Street, and showed us the newspaper report. The descriptions of the two men showed clearly who they really were. Justice had come at last to Murillo and Lopez.

"It hasn't been a very neat case, Watson," said Holmes later. "But everything seems clear now, doesn't it?"

"I still don't understand why that cook returned to Wisteria Lodge," I said.

"There are some strange religions in the State of San Pedro. Watson. Perhaps you have heard of one called Voodooism? Look it up in that encyclopedia."

I found the letter 'V' and read the article. The most important part was the following:

"In Voodooism certain special sacrifices must be made to please the gods. The usual sacrifices are a white bird, which is torn to pieces while it is still alive, and a black goat, whose throat is cut and whose body is burned."

I looked up. "But what about the leathery black baby that we found?" I asked.

"Oh, that was only one of the cook's gods," replied Holmes.

# Questions

## Questions on factual details

### The Red-Headed League

1  At the beginning of the story, how did Sherlock Holmes show his extraordinary cleverness?
2  What was unusual about Mr Wilson's assistant?
3  Why did Mr Wilson go to Pope's Court, and what happened there?
4  Why did he come to see Sherlock Holmes?
5  How did Holmes's behaviour at Saxe-Coburg Square puzzle Doctor Watson?
6  What was it that gave Mr Merryweather a surprise when he went into the cellar of the bank?
7  Who was "Vincent Spaulding" really, and what was he trying to do?

### The Man with the Twisted Lip

1  Why did Mrs Whitney come to see the Watsons?
2  What was the surprise that Watson had at the Bar of Gold?
3  What happened to Mrs Saint Clair in Upper Swandam Street?
4  Who was the chief suspect in the murder or disappearance of Neville Saint Clair, and why?
5  When Holmes met Mrs Saint Clair he expressed an opinion which later turned out to be mistaken. What was it?
6  What had Bradstreet noticed about his prisoner's appearance and habits?
7  Why did Neville Saint Clair give up his job as a newspaper reporter?

### The Engineer's Thumb

1  Why did Watson have to get up unusually early one morning in 1889?

2   Why did Captain Stark suddenly rush to the door of Mr Hatherley's office and throw it open?

3   What did Hatherley have to do in return for the fifty pounds?

4   What was surprising about this sum?

5   What did Hatherley discover about the hydraulic press when he went back inside it?

6   How did he escape from Captain Stark?

7   Why did Holmes choose the centre of Bradstreet's circle on the map as the most likely place?

8   What criminal trade were Stark and Ferguson engaged in?

## The Resident Patient

1   Why did Doctor Trevelyan's face go red when he met Holmes and Watson?

2   What offer did Mr Blessington make to Doctor Trevelyan?

3   How did Mr Blessington behave after he became Doctor Trevelyan's resident patient?

4   What discovery so upset Mr Blessington after the second visit of the two "Russian noblemen"?

5   What did Holmes learn from his questioning of Blessington?

6   What did the cigar ends show Holmes?

7   Who were the murderers, and why did they kill Blessington?

## The Disappearance of Lady Frances Carfax

1   In what way was Lady Frances like a chicken among wild animals?

2   Who was Miss Dobney, and why did she call Sherlock Holmes in?

3   What conclusion did Watson come to about the Lady Frances Carfax mystery as a result of his visits to Lausanne and Baden-Baden?

4   Who was the "French workman" in Montpellier, and what did he do for Watson?

5   What was Philip Green's true purpose in following Lady Frances through France and Germany?

6    Back in London, Holmes told Mr Green that he "feared the worst". What exactly did he mean?

7    What was the vital point that Holmes didn't understand until it was almost too late?


## The Three Garridebs

1    How did Sherlock Holmes know that "Mr John Garrideb" had been in England for some time?

2    Why, according to "John Garrideb", was he looking for two other men with the same surname?

3    How did Holmes make absolutely sure that the American was lying about where he came from?

4    How did Holmes know that the person living in the Little Ryder Street flat really was named Garrideb?

5    What reason did the American give for wanting Mr Nathan Garrideb to go off to Birmingham?

6    How did Holmes know that there was something wrong with the advertisement in the Birmingham newspaper?

7    How did Holmes succeed in trapping 'Killer' Evans?


## The Adventure of Wisteria Lodge

1    Why couldn't Mr Scott Eccles go to the police about his "strange and unpleasant" experience?

2    What crime did the police officer Gregson at first suspect Scott Eccles of committing, and why?

3    Why was Scott Eccles relieved to be able to go off to bed on the evening of his visit to Mr Garcia?

4    What puzzling contradiction was there about the time of the murder?

5    Why did Holmes ask the house agents for a list of all the big houses near Wisteria Lodge?

6    Who was Mr Henderson really, and why did his daughters' teacher hate him so much?

7    Who killed Garcia?

## *Questions on the stories as a whole*

1 Describe the personal qualities of two or three of the characters in "The Red-Headed League" (for example their intelligence, honesty, and courage).

2 In what way is the main villain in the "Red-Headed League" affair unusual? Describe his personality and background.

3 Describe Mr Wilson's job in Pope's Court, and say whether you would like to have such a job yourself.

4 What does Sherlock Holmes mean when he says that the explanation of Neville Saint Clair's disappearance is "in this bag"? Describe the circumstances in which he makes this remark.

5 Neville Saint Clair chose to earn money as a beggar rather than as a journalist. What do you think of his decision?

6 Is "The Man with the Twisted Lip" a story with (a) a happy ending, and (b) a moral? Explain your answers to both parts of the question.

7 How does Sherlock Holmes show his superior cleverness in "The Engineer's Thumb"?

8 In "The Resident Patient" how do (a) Mr "Blessington" and (b) his murderers make use of medical knowledge, or knowledge about the medical profession, for non-medical purposes?

9 Explain how in "The Resident Patient" Holmes shows that he is a better detective than the police officer Lanner.

10 Describe the scene in "The Disappearance of Lady Frances Carfax" that you find the most striking or dramatic, and say why you chose it.

11 Explain the method used by 'Holy' Peters and Annie Fraser in their attempt to get rid of Lady Frances for ever.

12 Tell the story of "The Disappearance of Lady Frances Carfax" as if you were Philip Green.

13 Who was "John Garrideb" really, and why did he invent the story of Alexander Hamilton Garrideb and his will?

14  What do we learn from "The Three Garridebs", and also from some of the other short stories in this book, about the relationship between Sherlock Holmes and Doctor Watson?

15  Compare the plot of "The Three Garridebs" with that of "The Red-Headed League" in as much detail as possible. Which story do you prefer, and why?

16  Describe the unusual households of Wisteria Lodge and High Gable.

17  What contrasts between English life and people and non-English ones can be found in "The Adventure of Wisteria Lodge"? Does the story give you any impression of Doyle's own attitude to people of different nationalities?

18  How does Doyle "punish" the villains of "The Adventure of Wisteria Lodge", and also those of some of the other villains in this book? Do they all get what they deserve, in your opinion?

19  What impression do you get from these stories of the characters and relationship of Sherlock Holmes and Doctor Watson?

20  Which one of the seven stories do you like or dislike most, and why?

# *Glossary*

**addict** a person who is unable to free him- or herself from a harmful habit, especially of taking drugs

**bandage** a long, narrow piece of material used for tying round a wound; **to bandage** = to tie up or round with a bandage.

**bow** to bend the head or upper part of the body forward, as a way of showing respect

**brandy** a strong alcoholic drink made from wine

**cab** (in former times)  a horse-drawn carriage for hire

**carpenter** a person who makes and repairs wooden objects as a job

**catalepsy** an illness in which a person can no longer control the movement of their body and their limbs remain in whatever position they are placed, or become stiff as in death

**cellar** an underground room used for storing goods

**chloroform** a colourless strong-smelling chemical which is used to make people unconscious

**cigar**  a roll of tobacco leaves for smoking, usually larger and more expensive than a cigarette

**client** a person who gets help and advice from a professional person

**clue** something that helps to find an answer to a question or mystery

**coffin** the box in which a dead person is buried

**cripple** someone who is unable to use one or more of their limbs properly, especially the legs

**encyclopedia** a book, or set of books, dealing with every branch of knowledge

**forger** a person who makes copies of money, papers, etc.

**fuller's earth** a kind of earth with various industrial and medical uses

**handcuffs** a pair of metal rings joined together by a short chain and fastened together with a key used for holding a criminal's wrists

**hydraulic** concerning or moved by the pressure of water or other liquids

**inn** a small hotel

**landlady** a woman from whom someone rents a room, house, etc.

**league** a group of people who have joined together to protect or improve their position

**magnifying glass** a piece of glass, curved on one or both sides, which makes things look larger than they really are when they are seen through it

**opium** a sleep-producing drug smoked for the strange dreams it is thought to cause

**patient** a person receiving medical treatment from a doctor

**pawnbroker** a person to whom people bring valuable articles so that he or she will lend them money, and who has the right to sell the articles if the money is not repaid within a certain time

**penny** a unit of money in Britain; in former times there were 240 pennies in one pound (now there are 100)

**resident** living (in a place)

**sacrifice** a religious offering to God or a god

**Scotland Yard** the main office of the London police

**search warrant** a written order given by a court to allow someone, usually the police, to search a place

**sill** a flat piece at the base of an opening or frame

**sleeve** a part of a garment for covering an arm

**straw** dried stems of plants, such as wheat

**suspicion** a belief that someone may be guilty or that something bad may exist; **suspicious** = causing one to suspect guilt; suspecting guilt

**swollen** increased beyond the usual size

**tattoo** a picture or message put on the skin by pricking with a needle and then pouring in coloured dyes

**telegram** a message sent by electrical signals along a wire

**undertaker** a person whose job is to arrange funerals

**veil** a covering of thin material for the head or face, worn by women

**will** an official statement of the way someone wants their property to be shared out after they die

Glossary compiled by Briqit Viney